"I'm not looking for any commitments right now, either," said Casey. *"Just not the right time.*

"For a pet," he added.

Natalie looked at him through her lashes. "So you think we'll be able to find a home for him?"

"I'm sure we will." He brushed a strand of hair away from her face. "Don't worry so much about it. He's pretty good at taking care of himself."

"I know." She glanced up at him.

He toyed with the ends of her hair around her face, then touched her mouth with one finger, teasing her lips apart.

A faint flush tinged her cheeks. He felt his own pulse beating as his body reacted to the nearness of hers. He wanted to tell her how beautiful she was, but he couldn't think of a way to do so without sounding trite or clichéd. He hoped she could see the sentiment in his eyes as he lowered his mouth to hers....

Dear Reader,

One of my very favorite places to get away for a few days is eastern Tennessee, in the beautiful Great Smoky Mountains. I love walking down wooded trails along rushing streams, watching birds and wildlife. It's so easy to leave the frenzied schedules and bothersome worries of everyday life behind when walking in a gentle mountain breeze accompanied by the sounds of nature.

After attending an east Tennessee wedding recently with my daughter, I knew I wanted to set another story there. I always enjoy revisiting the Walker family I introduced years ago in the FAMILY FOUND series, so I decided it was time to do a little matchmaking for yet another Walker son. Young attorney Casey Walker has a lot of troubles to leave behind when he takes temporary refuge in the Smoky Mountains, as does Natalie Lofton, the enigmatic woman he meets there. I hope you enjoy the story of how love—and the Smoky Mountain air—can heal the hearts of these two troubled soul mates.

Gina Wilkins

THE TEXAN'S TENNESSEE ROMANCE

GINA WILKINS

Silhouette®

SPECIAL EDITION®

Published by Silhouette Books

America's Publisher of Contemporary Romance

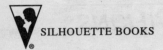

SILHOUETTE BOOKS

Recycling programs
for this product may
not exist in your area.

ISBN-13: 978-0-373-65436-9
ISBN-10:   0-373-65436-7

THE TEXAN'S TENNESSEE ROMANCE

Printed in U.S.A.

GINA WILKINS

is a bestselling and award-winning author who has written more than seventy novels for Harlequin and Silhouette Books. She credits her successful career in romance to her long, happy marriage and her three "extraordinary" children.

A lifelong resident of central Arkansas, Ms. Wilkins sold her first story to Harlequin Books in 1987 and has been writing full-time since. She has appeared on the Waldenbooks, B. Dalton and *USA TODAY* bestseller lists. She is a three-time recipient of the Maggie Award for Excellence, sponsored by Georgia Romance Writers, and has won several awards from the reviewers of *Romantic Times BOOKreviews*.

As always, for my family:
John, Courtney, Kerry, Justin and David.

Chapter One

He was quite possibly one of the worst maintenance men Natalie Lofton had ever seen. Pretty, but incompetent. Watching as he fumbled with a leaky pipe under her kitchen sink, she wondered where on earth her aunt and uncle had found this twenty-something guy, who had introduced himself only as Casey. She couldn't imagine what had made them think he was qualified to be a handyman for the vacation cabins they owned in the Smoky Mountains around Gatlinburg, Tennessee.

"Is there anything I can do to help you?" she asked the third time she heard an ominous clang followed by a muttered curse.

Her voice from the doorway must have startled him. She saw his nice backside jerk, heard what sounded like a painful thump from beneath the sink and then yet another colorful expletive, bitten off midway.

He emerged ruefully rubbing a spot on the top of his head, and she couldn't help noticing again that he was certainly good-looking. His appearance, she decided, defied simple, one-word adjectives. His hair was just a shade more brown than blond, and his almost-crystalline-bright eyes looked blue one moment, green the next. His jawline was sharply carved, but flashing dimples softened his cheeks. She suspected his personality was just as multifaceted.

"What did you say?" he asked.

She moved closer, bending over to see what he'd been doing under there. How much time did it take to replace a leaky trap, anyway? "I asked if there's anything I can do to help."

"Thanks, but I've got it. It won't be much longer."

"Uh-huh." She hoped she didn't sound as skeptical as she felt.

His polite smile fading, he ducked back under the sink, flipping over to lie on his back this time. She couldn't help noticing that he looked just as good from waist down as he did above. Long legs, flat stomach, nice…

"Could you hand me that wrench, please? The big one?"

She picked up the biggest wrench she saw in his box and leaned over to hand it to him. "This one?"

"Yeah, thanks."

She watched as he fitted it to the pipe. "Um, don't you think you should—"

"What?" he asked loudly, unable to hear from beneath the sink. Even as he spoke, he gave the wrench a big twist. She saw the wrench slip, smashing through the thin copper water pipe next to him.

Cold water sprayed in a geyser from the broken pipe, hitting her squarely in the face. Gasping, she heard Casey sputter as he lay at the bottom of a veritable waterfall. While she stumbled backward, he scrambled frantically clanging and muttering until he reduced the gushing to a dribble by turning off the water valve.

"—shut off the water supply?" she finished her question in a grumble.

"I am so sorry," he said, awkwardly climbing from beneath the sink. He was even wetter than Natalie, if that was possible. His light brown hair dripped around his face, and his blue polo shirt was plastered to his well-defined chest.

Which reminded her…

Glancing downward, she noted that her thin, yellow cotton shirt had molded itself to her, going almost transparent when wet. She grabbed hold of the front, pulling the fabric away from her body. "I'll go find some towels."

He raised his gaze quickly to her face. "Yeah, okay. I'm really sorry."

She nodded and darted out of the kitchen, heading straight for the cabin's only bedroom. She wasn't bringing towels to him until she had changed her shirt.

Catching a glimpse of herself in the antique oval mirror over the rustic dresser, she groaned. Water trickled from the ends of her chin-length, honey-blond, angled bob. The bare minimum of makeup she'd applied that morning was water-splotched. And her now-transparent shirt made it very clear that she'd donned a comfy—and very thin—nude-toned bra that morning.

She changed quickly into a dry, slightly thicker bra and a dark blue, scoop-neck T-shirt. Deciding her jeans weren't damp enough to change, she ran a brush through her wet hair. After dusting a little powder over her now-shiny face, she grabbed an armload of towels and headed back toward the kitchen where surely the world's worst handyman waited for her.

Way to go, Casey. Drench one of the tenants. The owner's niece, to make it even worse. Some handyman you are.

Of course, that was the problem. He wasn't a handyman at all. Just a twenty-six-year-old man in the middle of an identity crisis.

"Here." Reentering the room, Natalie tossed a fluffy white towel to him. "Dry yourself. I'll start on the floor."

He draped the towel over his head and rubbed his soaked hair, then dragged it over his neck and the front of his shirt. While he did so, he watched Natalie kneel to swab up the water pooled on the oak floor. She'd changed clothes, he noted. He tried to push away a lingering image of her wet, yellow shirt plastered to very nice curves.

"I'll have to install a new pipe. And the flooring of the cabinet needs to be replaced," he said. "The slow leak you found has pretty much rotted it out."

"The fast leak you created didn't help any, either," she muttered, gathering wet towels to carry into the small laundry room attached to the kitchen.

He supposed he deserved that. But it rather annoyed him, anyway. Especially since he'd broken the damn pipe because she'd distracted him and made him self-conscious by watching him and talking to him while he was trying to work. Serious control issues, this one.

As if she'd read a hint of his thoughts in his eyes, she grimaced slightly. "Sorry," she said, pushing a damp strand of hair off her cheek. "I know it was an accident."

"Yeah. But you're right. I didn't help matters much," he conceded, softened by her apology. No matter how grudgingly she'd offered it.

"How long have you worked for Uncle Mack?" she asked, glancing at the tool box beside his feet.

"Just over a week now."

"And how long have you been a handyman?"

"Maintenance facilitator," he corrected her with a grin. When she only looked at him, he shrugged and said, "Just over a week now."

"Oh." She looked as though she'd like to ask a few more questions, but either manners or lack of sufficient interest kept her from doing so. Whatever the reason, he was relieved that she kept her questions to herself.

There were a few things he would like to know about her, too. But this wasn't the time. He reached down for his tools. "I'm going to have to get a new copper pipe to replace the one I broke. Might have to get some help changing it out. I'm afraid you're going to be without water in here for a few hours, but you still have water in the bathroom."

She nodded. "Aunt Jewel told me the cabin is undergoing renovations and repair work. That's why she's letting me use it while I—for now," she corrected herself. "I can get by without the kitchen sink for a while."

"Okay. Well then, I'll be back later," he said, moving toward the door. "Sorry again about—you know." He motioned toward her still damp hair, then let himself out of the cabin before he made a bigger fool of himself.

Which wouldn't be easy to do, he thought as he climbed into the black SUV parked in the gravel driveway. He hadn't exactly wowed Natalie with his maintenance skills. No wonder she had wanted to know how long he'd been doing this.

Because it was the first week in November, the fall colors had begun to fade, and the leaves were already beginning to drop. It wasn't cold yet, but a nip in the air promised that it would be soon. Driving down the winding mountain road that ran alongside one of the many rushing creeks in the area, Casey noted the signs of approaching winter, even as he wondered what Natalie would have said if he'd told her the whole truth about himself.

He'd been doing a few maintenance chores for the past week, but he was actually an associate attorney in a high-powered, Dallas law firm. One of the youngest ever hired by the firm, starting right after earning his law degree when he was only twenty-four.

The six-week leave of absence he'd taken almost two weeks ago hadn't exactly cemented his future with the firm. No one but his cousin Molly Reeves understood or approved of his need to take that time now to reevaluate his life and the future that had been laid out for him almost from birth. Molly and her husband, Kyle, partners in Mack and Jewel McDooley's vacation property management business, had given him a place to stay during the hiatus, and the space he needed to deal with his issues.

As payment for their hospitality, he'd volunteered to fill in for the regular full-time handyman, who'd been in a car accident recently and wouldn't be able to work for at least another month. Molly had been understandably skeptical about his offer. She knew he hadn't spent a lot of time working with his hands while he'd concentrated on school for most of his life. But he'd convinced her and the others that he could handle some simple repair work.

And darned if he hadn't messed up for the first time right in front of the owner's niece, he thought with a scowl. Not only that—the owner's very hot niece.

He didn't know what he'd been expecting when Mack mentioned that his wife's niece was staying in one of the cabins for a few weeks, but the woman he'd met that morning had taken him by surprise. Tall and classy, she was a cool blond with warm chocolate eyes. Her age was hard to guess, but he'd estimated a little older than himself. The extra couple of years looked good on her.

She'd even held on to her dignity for the most part when he'd doused her with cold water from beneath the sink. He could still see her standing there, dripping, her wet shirt clinging to her like a second skin, her expression more exasperated than angry. He doubted that she would have appreciated knowing the thoughts that had gone through his mind at that moment, though he'd tried very hard to rein them in.

He wondered what her story was. All he'd been told was that she was taking a quiet, solitary vacation while she was between jobs. He hadn't been informed, nor had he asked, what she did for a living or what she might be hiding from in her isolated mountain retreat.

He shook his head impatiently, bringing the speculation to an abrupt end. Just because *he* had issues that had sent him running to the mountains to brood and reevaluate his life didn't mean everyone else was in the same boat. Maybe Natalie just wanted to take advantage of a free vacation in her relatives' under-renovation cabin.

And maybe he was going to sprout wings and fly. He didn't know Natalie Lofton or the details of her current situation, but the studied calm of her demeanor hadn't completely hidden the storm in her deep brown eyes. That was one of his talents—reading other people's emotions, no matter how hard they tried to keep them hidden. The skill had served him well in his law career, giving him an edge that he had never hesitated to exploit.

So while he might not know what was eating at Natalie, he knew something was. And he suspected that she wouldn't be averse to taking her frustration out on the less-than-proficient handyman.

* * *

Casey returned just after lunch. Natalie let him back in, noting that he'd brought help this time. "Hello, Kyle," she greeted the second man.

A hard-carved ex-soldier in his mid-thirties, Kyle Reeves had been the McDooleys' business partner for almost five years. Their late son, Tommy—Natalie's favorite cousin in her childhood—had been Kyle's best friend. They had served in the military together for several years, until a roadside bomb in the Middle East had ended Tommy's life and almost killed Kyle at the same time.

It had taken Kyle a long time to recover, both physically and emotionally. He still walked with a slight limp and had a few faintly visible scars, which only added to his rough appeal.

Because Kyle had no family of his own, Mack and Jewel had taken him in. They had given him encouragement and support and had found in him a reason to put aside their grief and focus on someone else who needed them. He had become a surrogate son to them, and Natalie had no question that they loved him like one. Nor did she doubt that Kyle would willingly die for either of the couple who had given him a reason to keep living when, from what she had surmised, he'd been all too close to giving up.

Kyle returned her greeting with a nod. "How's it going, Natalie? You comfortable here?"

"Very much so, thank you. It's a lovely cabin."

"It will be when we've finished the renovations." He glanced at Casey with a wry half smile. "And if I can keep my cousin-in-law, here, from flooding the place."

"Cousin-in-law?" she repeated, glancing at Casey, who stood quietly behind the man who was probably his senior by a decade. "You're Molly's cousin?"

He nodded. "On my father's side. My last name is Walker, which was Molly's maiden name."

"I didn't realize." But it explained a lot, she decided. She knew now how he'd gotten the job.

He grinned as though he had somehow read her thoughts. "Gotta love nepotism, right?"

Her lips twitched with a smile she had a hard time containing. At least he admitted he hadn't been hired for his maintenance skills.

"Molly told me to ask you to dinner," Kyle said, shifting a heavy toolbox in his left hand. "Maybe Friday night?"

Though she still wasn't feeling very social, it seemed ungracious to decline. "I'd like that. Tell her I said thank you."

He nodded again. "She'll be pleased. Since Micah was born, she hasn't been able to get out much. She spends a lot of time with the kids and with Jewel, but she'll enjoy having someone new to talk with for a change."

Because she'd been so busy with her career the past few years, Natalie hadn't been able to visit her aunt and uncle much. She had met Molly only a few times, but she liked Kyle's bubbly, redheaded wife quite a bit. The young mother of three-year-old Olivia and two-month-old Micah had an infectious smile and an inviting Texas drawl. She seemed to have a knack for putting people at ease within minutes of meeting her. She had certainly done so with Natalie.

Leaving the men to work in the big, eat-in kitchen, Natalie returned to the bedroom she'd been sleeping in since she'd arrived four nights ago. This was the only real bedroom, though the couch in the large living room was a sleeper that pulled out into a queen-sized bed. The cabin had two bathrooms, a smaller one with a shower off the living room, and the master bathroom with a shower-tub combo. The master bath was also being renovated during this off-season remodel. A new toilet, sink and countertop had already been installed. There was no mirror in the bathroom now, though she could see that one had hung above the sink.

She'd been told that a new mirror would be installed within the next few days. In the meantime, she was able to use the mirror over the bedroom dresser for applying her makeup and doing her hair.

Like the rest of the small, older vacation cabin, the bedroom decor was country casual. A big iron bed was covered with a hand-pieced quilt for a bedspread and lots of comfy pillows. Matching oak nightstands topped with a pair of antique lamps sat on either side of the bed. Country prints hung on the log walls. What appeared to be homemade lace curtains framed the window that looked out over the mountaintops. Too bad she hadn't been able to really appreciate the stunning view while she'd been here.

Her laptop sat on the tiny writing desk in one corner of the room. The screen saver had activated, and colorful animated fish swam across the screen. She'd always wanted a real aquarium, but her demanding career had taken so much of her time that she wouldn't have been able to maintain or enjoy one.

She had time for an aquarium now, she thought glumly. Not that she would be able to afford one once her savings were depleted, as they would be rather quickly if the private investigator she had hired recently didn't come up with some answers soon.

A flick of the wireless mouse made the screen saver disappear, replaced by a list of her former associates in the large Nashville law firm where she had worked for the past four-and-a-half years. It was a lengthy list—thirty-five members, seventy-five associates, and fifteen staff attorneys, which didn't even count all the clerical staff. A big firm. A lot of suspects. And she could rule out only about half of them. She wondered if Rand Beecham, the rather eccentric P.I., had had any more success in the week that had passed since her last update from him.

She heard a clang from the kitchen, and a curse that sounded like Casey's voice, followed by a quick laugh that might have come from Kyle. She glanced that way, then looked back at the names on her screen, her slight smile fading. Someone on this list had set her up, framed her for leaking confidential client information to the media in return for under-the-table payments. Because of that untrue accusation, she had lost a position she'd spent several long, hard years working to achieve. Until she proved her innocence, her career—her very life—was on hold.

"So, when are you coming home?"

Leaning back in a patio chair on the deck of the tiny, A-frame cabin in which he was staying—one of the two cabins currently under renovation and not rented during this off-peak season, the other being Natalie's—Casey gazed at the wooded path stretched in front of him, and tried to come up with a satisfactory answer to his cousin's question. "I don't know, exactly," he said into the cell phone he held to his ear. "A couple more weeks, maybe."

"You've been there almost two weeks already," Aaron Walker complained. "What are you doing there all this time?"

"Kyle and Mack are renovating two of their vacation cabins during the off season, and I volunteered to give them a hand."

"You're doing carpentry work?" Aaron made no effort to hide his skepticism.

"Yeah. And a little plumbing. Some painting. Cleaning gutters. That sort of thing."

"You. Plumbing. That can't be good."

Casey was glad Aaron couldn't see him wince as he remembered the way he'd soaked Natalie with a spray of cold water. Wouldn't Aaron and his twin, Andrew, have gotten unholy delight out of that scene? Not to mention their slightly older cousin, Jason, who was always commenting on the younger trio's proclivity for trouble.

Maybe he'd tell them about his first real attempt at plumbing sometime. But not now. "I'm doing okay. Kyle said I've been a lot of help."

"Yeah, well, you've had your vacation and you've gotten to play with tools. So, don't you think it's time to come home now? Everybody's asking about you. And this hiatus can't look good to the powers that be at your firm. If it weren't for the family connections, there's no way they'd have let a junior associate take off this long without repercussions."

Casey scowled in response to the reminder of those "family connections." It was true that his paternal aunt Michelle D'Alessandro was one of the firm's wealthiest and most prestigious clients. And that his maternal grandfather was a nationally known and admired prosecutor in Chicago, who'd roomed with the senior partner in Casey's Dallas firm years ago back in their college days and had maintained that friendship ever since. And that Casey's father was a partner in the largest and most respected private investigation and security company in Dallas and his mother the CEO of an acclaimed accounting firm. All of which might have gotten him hired in the first place, but he'd worked damned hard to justify that decision. He'd earned every dollar of his generous paychecks.

At least, he'd thought so until he'd lost the first truly high-profile case he'd been assigned. Not only had it been a defeat, it had been a particularly painful, public and humiliating one. His friends and family had rallied around him, assuring him that every attorney suffered losses, but there had been more than a few in the Dallas legal community who had taken great pleasure in seeing "the wonderboy," as they had dubbed him, taken down a few pegs.

A week after that loss, he had suffered a second career blow. Only that time, at the hands of an arrogant young man Casey had successfully defended in a previous charge, an innocent person had died. And Casey still wondered if he was at least partially to blame for that tragedy.

"I just needed some time off," he insisted to his cousin. "I haven't had a break in—well, ever. Working every summer during high school and college, straight into law school, and from there directly into the job at the firm. I always meant to take a vacation, but the time never seemed to be right."

"And you think it's right now?" Aaron asked skeptically. "After—well, you know?"

"After I lost the Parmenter case, you mean? Yeah. I think I need this vacation now more than I've ever needed it before."

There was a long pause, and then Aaron spoke again, an uncharacteristic note of caution in his voice. "Um, I suppose you've heard that Tamara and Fred have been getting a lot of face time around town lately?"

"Yeah, I heard they've been seen together at every highbrow event in Dallas for the past few weeks. And that they have an uncanny talent for being in exactly the right place every time a flashbulb goes off so their picture makes the society pages the next day."

"Carly said she and Richard attended a charity thing this past weekend and Tamara was there flashing a doorknob-sized diamond ring. No official engagement has been announced, but…well, Carly said Tamara was looking very much like a canary-eating cat."

"That I can believe."

"So, uh, if they are engaged—how do you feel about that?"

"Honestly, I don't care. If Tamara wants to marry Fred, more power to her. I hope they'll have a great life with a couple of McMansions, two perfect kids, and a permanent spot on the social registry. That's what she always dreamed of."

"And she thought she was going to get there with you."

"I guess. Until she decided that Fred will get her there faster, already being a partner in a rival firm and all."

She had made that decision, at least openly, right after Casey's big courtroom loss. Apparently, she'd been debating it for some time before that. And she had explored her options by seeing Fred behind Casey's back, a juicy tidbit that had been discussed in the break rooms and around the water coolers for several weeks before Tamara had bothered to bring him into the loop. She had done so with a blunt announcement that their long-standing, though unofficial, engagement was at an end.

It took a great deal of effort, sacrifice and ruthless calculation to make it to the very peak of the social heap, she had informed him entirely without irony. She had at first thought he was willing to invest himself fully in that mission, but lately she'd been having doubts. She had no such reservations about Fred, who cared every bit as much about status and image as she did.

"You really should come home," Aaron urged again, breaking into Casey's grim memories. "Be seen around town with a couple of hot women. Andy and I just happen to know a few to introduce you to. Show Tamara, and everyone else, that you're not sitting around pining for her. Get back to work, win a couple of big cases, prove you've still got the stuff, which we all know you do. Have some fun, raise some hell on the weekends. Just like the old days, you know?"

Casey knew what "old days" his cousin referred to. In their

teens, he and the twins had been known in the family as "the terrible trio" because of the lengths they had gone to in pursuit of a good time. Practical jokes, daredevil escapades, impulsive road trips. Weekends had been their time to raise some hell. And they had excelled at that as much as they had in their separate educational pursuits.

"I'll be home soon," he said, unwilling to commit any more than that. "Besides, Molly and Kyle really do need my assistance for a little while longer. Their regular maintenance guy won't be back for several more weeks. Kyle and Mack stay busy all the time trying to keep up and it helps that I can do some of the easier stuff. Gives Kyle a little more time to spend with Molly and the kids."

He knew that was one argument Aaron would have a hard time contesting. All the cousins had a soft spot for Molly. Not to mention that family always came first for the entire Walker clan, so giving a father more time with his wife, toddler daughter and infant son would be something they'd all consider worth the effort.

Sure enough, Aaron didn't seem to know quite what to say, except "Well, try not to destroy anything there, okay? You're a lawyer, not a carpenter. And don't stay too long. Frankly, I seem to be more worried about your career than you are."

"Says the guy who is thinking of making a big job change."

"That's because I don't like what I'm doing now. That isn't true for you."

"Yeah. Um. Right."

They disconnected a few minutes later on a pleasant enough note, though Aaron's warnings about Casey's possible career jeopardy had left Casey feeling tense and irritable. To distract himself, he settled more comfortably in his chair and focused on the beauty of the wooded hillsides around him. And then he realized that an even more appealing picture had taken shape in his mind—Natalie Lofton, standing wet and startled in front of him, her thin, almost-transparent shirt revealing just enough to make his pulse race.

He was a bit surprised by the clarity of the mental image. His life was in enough turmoil right now, he told himself. He didn't need an inconvenient attraction to a woman who seemed to be in as much of a quandary as he was.

Or maybe that was exactly what he needed, he mused, tugging thoughtfully at his lower lip. Hadn't Aaron just said that he should start seeing other women, forget about Tamara, put his troubles out of his mind? Which meant he should be open to possibilities as he worked on the cabin in which Natalie was staying.

He would be seeing her again, he thought with a buzz of anticipation. Soon.

Chapter Two

Casey Walker was in Natalie's cabin again, this time in her bedroom.

Sitting at the round oak table in the kitchen with her computer in front of her, Natalie could hear him banging around as he removed the wobbly old ceiling fan and prepared to install another. She hadn't been able to resist expressing her concern about his ability to handle that task, but he'd scowled and assured her that he knew what he was doing. He and Kyle had installed a new fan in one of the other cabins only the day before, he'd informed her.

When he finished replacing the fan, he was going to hang the new mirror in the bathroom. He planned to accomplish both those tasks before he left today.

Listening to the unnerving noises coming from the back of the cabin, Natalie wondered if Kyle was investing too much confidence in his wife's cousin.

She had offered to help, but Casey had politely declined. She suspected that he hadn't wanted her watching him. At least he'd had the foresight to turn off the electricity to the back part of the cabin, so he was working in the sunlight streaming through the big bedroom window.

She'd just happened to observe, of course, that he looked very good standing in that sunlight, which brought out the gold strands in his blondish-brown hair.

Frowning, she turned her attention back to the monitor in front of her. It showed how frustrating this research was that she was so easily distracted by the sight of a young stud in a tool belt. Hadn't she learned her lesson when Thad had been so eager to distance himself from her after the humiliating debacle at her law firm? Great-looking young guys were always on the prowl, hunting for a good time, but quick to disappear whenever any sign of trouble cropped up.

So maybe she'd noticed Casey looking at her when he thought she wouldn't see, and maybe she was aware of a muted sizzle between them. Maybe she would have been intrigued by the possibility of a careful holiday flirtation if it hadn't been for the cloud hanging over her head. As it was, she had neither the time nor the energy to give in to impulse now. Or at least she tried to convince herself of that, even as she savored another mental image of the way Casey looked in his soft work shirt and weathered jeans.

Maybe she had a *little* extra time…

A particularly loud thump from the back room made her start. After a momentary internal debate, she rose and moved that way, half expecting to find pieces of ceiling scattered across the floor of the bedroom.

Casey glanced around when she stopped in the doorway.

The old ceiling fan sat on the floor at his feet, entirely in one piece as far as she could tell. Wires dangled from the fixture in the ceiling, but it seemed that everything was under control.

"Sorry," he said. "I set it down a bit more heavily than I intended. I hope I didn't distract you from anything important."

Oh, he distracted her, all right. She just didn't think it was a good idea to let him know that. "No, I was just checking to see if you need any assistance. Maybe I could help you hold the new fan while you install it?"

"Actually, Kyle showed me how to balance it while I connect everything. It's just a small, fairly lightweight fan. But thanks for the offer."

She nodded. "I'll be in the kitchen if you need me for anything."

"Okay, thanks."

Back at the kitchen table, she stared again at the long list of names on her computer monitor. During the past thirty-six hours, she had shortened the list of suspects. By two names. Both of whom were dead. And she'd gotten to the point that she wasn't even entirely sure of *their* innocence. She hoped Beecham would call her today. If not, she was going to try to reach him and ask if he'd made any further progress with his investigation. She was certainly making no headway with her own.

Disgusted with herself, with the entire situation, she pushed the computer away with a low growl. A beeping sound made her pull it back again.

Hey, Nat. U there?

The instant message had popped up on her screen from a sender whose screen name was "GlitRChik" and whose avatar was a slightly crazed-looking fairy.

I'm here, Natalie typed back. What's up?

Been doing some snooping.

Natalie replied quickly, Call me on my cell, Amber. Don't put anything in writing.

Sorry

A moment later, Natalie's cell phone chimed. She lifted it to her ear with only a perfunctory glance at the ID screen. "Hello."

"Hi, Nat."

"Don't write anything down," Natalie repeated firmly. "Especially on your computer. Maybe I'm being paranoid, but I think I have some reason to be concerned."

"I know you do," Amber Keller, Natalie's former assistant, sympathized. "I didn't think about IMs leaving a paper trail."

"They do. As I said, I'm probably being overly cautious, but still…what have you learned?"

"Not a lot," her friend and former subordinate confessed. "Just one sort of interesting tidbit."

"Which is?" Natalie prodded, even as a series of thumps sounded from the bedroom, making it hard to concentrate.

"Hang on a sec." She stood and moved toward the kitchen doorway, thinking she would hear better if she went outside to the big wooden deck attached to the back of the vacation cabin. Closing the door behind her, she let a brisk, late-autumn breeze toss her hair as she sank into a green-painted Adirondack chair. "Okay. Now. What interesting tidbit?"

"Cathy Linski just bought a new car. A pretty fancy one. Convertible."

Frowning, Natalie asked, "I'm sorry, I don't understand. What does that have to do with me?"

"Well, a month ago, Cathy was whining about not having

any money and being on the brink of bankruptcy. Now all of a sudden she's spending money like crazy. When someone asked her what's going on, she just laughed and said she came into a windfall and she's going to enjoy it while it lasts."

"Oh. That *is* interesting," Natalie murmured, following Amber's line of thought. She wondered if Beecham knew about this development.

"Yeah. It's not much to report—might have nothing at all to do with your situation—but I thought you'd want to know."

"That's all you have?"

"I'm afraid so. Everyone's been pretty closemouthed around here for the past couple of weeks. Nobody mentions you at all."

Natalie bit her lower lip, then released it with a slight sigh. "Okay. Thanks, Amber. Let me know if you hear anything else, okay?"

"You got it. I'd better get back to work. Steve's not nearly as tolerant as you were about personal time during the workday."

"Don't risk your job because of me. You can always call me when you get home. It's not like I'm doing anything else in the evenings."

"You want my advice? Try to have a little fun while you're there in the mountains. You've been working too hard for a couple of years. This is your first time off work in, like, forever. Surely there's some interesting guy there who can help you work off some frustration, if you know what I mean."

Natalie didn't have to ask for clarification. Amber thought there were few problems that couldn't be alleviated by a night of partying. A hard worker during the week, she was an equally zealous fun-seeker during the weekends. She'd nagged Natalie for months to join her at some of the wilder Nashville clubs on a Friday or Saturday night, promising a "hot time" that would make all the tension knots in her neck and shoulders mysteriously disappear. Amber couldn't understand why Natalie had been at all hesitant to accept.

At the time, Natalie had been worried about damaging her image as a serious, hardworking, ambitious attorney. Little had she known then that her reputation would soon take a much harder hit than if she'd merely been seen partying in a few clubs.

As for "some interesting guy"...she glanced toward the back door of the cabin, thinking of Casey, and knowing exactly how Amber would react if she could see him. She'd be all over the sexy maintenance man like "white on rice," as Aunt Jewel would say, and she'd think Natalie was crazy for not at least trying to flirt with the guy. But then, Amber wasn't in the process of fighting for her professional life, either.

"You'd better get back to work," she said, deciding not to address her friend's advice. "Thanks for calling."

"You bet. We're going to figure out who set you up this way, Nat," Amber said loyally. "And when we do, everybody's going to know about it. I'll make sure of that."

As she disconnected the call, Natalie wished there was some way she could let Amber know how much that support meant to her. So many of the people she had considered friends had dropped her like a hot potato after she was summarily fired from her position with the firm. They had been all too willing to believe she'd let greed trump ethics and had engaged in behavior that they should have realized was utterly foreign to her.

Unable to appreciate the nice weather or the beautiful scenery surrounding her, she closed her cell phone. Her lips felt dry and she realized she was thirsty. She'd stocked the fridge with her favorite bottled water. Rising, she moved toward the door, wondering idly if Casey had finished installing the fan yet.

He was standing at the sink when she entered the kitchen.

Though his back was turned to her, he seemed to be fumbling with the roll of paper towels on the counter.

"Can I help you with something?" she asked.

He started and turned toward her, his left hand cupped in front of him. Something about the way he held it made her study him more closely. Only then did she notice the blood that dripped from his palm.

Sighing lightly, she moved toward him. "What have you done now? Let me see."

If Casey'd had access to a teleporter, he would have beamed out of there right that minute. But since his sci-fi fandom was of no use to him just then, he squared his shoulders and tried to look nonchalant even though he was bleeding all over her kitchen.

"It's just a scratch," he assured her, closing his fist before she could see the wound. "I'll wash it off and wrap a paper towel around it until it scabs over and it'll be fine."

"You don't get that much blood from 'just a scratch,'" she argued, reaching for his wrist. "I think you should let me look at it."

"What are you, a doctor?" he asked, reluctantly opening his fingers.

"No, but I played one on TV," she answered absently, wincing as she looked at the ragged gash across his palm.

"Kidding," she added with a glance up at his face. "I'm not an actor. Casey, this is more than a scratch. How did you do it?"

Amused by her automatic quip—so he wasn't the only pop-culture fan in the room—he shrugged, having no intention of telling her exactly how he'd sliced himself. "Just carelessness. I really don't think it's all that bad."

She studied his palm again and the sight of her bent over his hand, peering so closely he could feel her warm breath on his skin, made an odd feeling go down his spine. At least, he assumed it was her closeness and not blood loss causing that sensation. He was a healthy, red-blooded—hah—young man, after all.

She glanced up at him again. "You're dripping blood all over my floor and you find it funny?" she asked a bit too politely.

He stifled his inappropriate grin, suspecting she wouldn't share his humor in the situation. "Sorry. I'll clean up the mess, of course."

"First, we're going to have to stop the bleeding." She tugged him toward the table. "Sit down. There's a first aid kit in the bathroom."

"I don't—"

She gave him a look that reminded him oddly of his mother's famous don't-argue-with-me expression. His libido effectively quashed, he sank into a chair.

She returned a few minutes later carrying a small, white plastic box which she set on the table and opened purposefully. He grimaced when he saw that the first item she removed was an alcohol pad. That was going to sting.

"When's the last time you had a tetanus shot?" she asked, ripping open the packet containing the pad.

"Last year. I cut myself on some rusty barbed wire at my cousin's ranch. Thought it was a good idea to have a tetanus shot after that."

She dabbed the cut with the pad and he had to make an effort not to grunt. He'd anticipated correctly. It stung.

"Are you always so accident-prone?"

He frowned. "Not really."

"Mmm." She didn't sound as if she entirely believed him.

He supposed he couldn't blame her, really. He'd sprayed her with water fixing a pipe and sliced open his hand installing a fan. She'd probably expect him to break a leg or something if he had to climb a ladder.

"I don't think you need stitches," she said, studying the now-clean wound, which was still oozing blood, though the bleeding had slowed.

"Definitely don't need stitches."

She pulled out a tube of ointment and an adhesive bandage. "At least let me cover it so it will stay clean."

He nodded, figuring that was a good idea.

Kneeling in front of him, she cradled his hand in hers as she carefully smoothed the ointment over his injury. She was wearing a thin, long-sleeved green sweater with a scoop neck. He realized that from this angle, he could see the creamy upper curves of her breasts. Any resemblance he'd seen in her to his mother disappeared. He lifted his gaze quickly to the window across the room before he embarrassed himself by visibly reacting to her crouching so close to him, looking like—well, like that, he thought with a fleeting glance back at her.

She looked up and met his eyes. "Am I hurting you?"

"No." Aware that he'd spoken rather curtly, he looked out the window again. "Almost done?"

"Yes. Just let me—" She spread the bandage across his palm, centered the gauze part over the wound, then pressed down on the adhesive edges to secure it. "There. How does that feel?"

At that moment he didn't feel a thing in his hand, though he was aware of plenty of sensations in other parts of him. Maybe the blood loss *had* affected him, he thought grimly, though he knew full well he hadn't been injured badly enough for that to be an issue. "It feels fine. Thanks. I'd better wipe up in here and then get back to work. I still have to hang that mirror in the bathroom."

"Are you sure you can work with that sore hand?"

"Oh, sure." He flexed his fingers a few times in demonstration, managing not to wince with the movement. "It's fine."

"Did you finish installing the fan?"

"Yeah." He had been cleaning up in there when he'd sliced himself with a box cutter while breaking down the fan's cardboard box. Maybe he'd been a little distracted by the sight of a lacy nightgown peeking out of the top of a drawer. He had no intention of telling her either how—or why—he'd sustained the injury. "I'll take care of this mess, and then I'll hang the mirror and get out of your way."

But she had already grabbed a paper towel and was scrubbing at the drops of blood on the countertop. "I've got this. You finish your work."

It was obvious that she wasn't one to be deterred once she'd made up her mind. Maybe she just wanted him to finish up and clear out quickly. Because it wasn't worth an argument, he merely nodded. "All right. Thanks."

She nodded in return, busily cleaning up the evidence of his latest act of clumsiness.

Shaking his head in self-reproof, he went back to her bedroom, suddenly wanting to be out of that cabin before his ego took an even harder hit. He seemed to feel that way every time he left Natalie, he thought with a rueful grimace.

Even as she drove the ten miles of winding roads down the mountain and into Gatlinburg early Friday evening, Natalie wished she could have found some reason to decline the dinner invitation that had brought her out of her solitude. Other than Casey and the one maintenance visit from Kyle, the only people Natalie had seen in the past week were her aunt and uncle. They'd popped in the day before to check on her and bring her a supply of Aunt Jewel's home cooking, though she had assured them that wasn't necessary.

She'd had phone calls, of course. Amber. Her dad. Her mom. All of them were worried about her, though only Amber and her father knew exactly why Natalie was no longer working for the firm in Nashville. She hadn't even told her aunt Jewel the whole story, not wanting to upset her.

She had assured her callers that she was fine. She needed this time away. She needed the rest. She needed to regroup emotionally and wanted privacy in which to do some research on her own, while the private investigator she'd hired from the yellow pages did some discreet snooping back in Nashville. Her father was the only one who knew she'd hired the P.I.

Had her father lived in Nashville—or even in the same country—he might have gotten a bit more involved in the fight to clear his daughter's name. But since he was currently working in the publishing industry in London, he'd been able to do little except offer long-distance advice and encouragement. Her mother, now married to a college professor in Oxford, Mississippi, tended to be more of a hand-wringer and worrier than a useful resource.

Natalie was pretty much on her own in this battle—but then, she was accustomed to taking care of herself. She'd done so since her parents had split up in a rather ugly divorce when she was eighteen.

Following the directions she'd been given, she parked in the driveway of Kyle and Molly's lovely Gatlinburg home. They'd bought the house soon after their marriage just over four years ago. Before that, Molly had lived on a ranch in Texas and Kyle in one of the cabins they now rented out to vacationers.

A brightly colored, plastic, three-wheel riding toy partially blocked the stone walkway. Bypassing it, Natalie stepped onto the long porch that fronted the yellow frame house with pristine white trim and shutters. The inviting porch seemed well utilized. A swing at one end was padded with yellow and green patterned cushions; two rocking chairs with matching cushions sat nearby. Big planters held vibrant autumn chrysanthemums, and a couple more toys peeked from behind one of those pots.

She pressed the doorbell. What sounded like a small dog immediately went into a frenzy of barking inside, and she sighed. She wasn't particularly fond of hyper, little purse puppies.

The door opened and Kyle greeted her with a slight smile. "Hi, Natalie. Did you have any trouble finding us?"

"Not a bit. Your directions were very good."

"Come on in. Be quiet, Poppy," he added with what sounded like weary resignation as he glanced down at the yapping brown-and-white Chihuahua at his feet.

"Sorry," he said when Natalie walked in. "The stupid dog thinks he's a Doberman. He doesn't actually bite, he just wants you to think he will."

"He? Didn't you call it Poppy?"

He chuckled wryly. "Olivia named him. She loves the little fleabag."

Poppy had already turned and ripped into another room, his job as guard dog apparently completed. Kyle gestured in the same direction, inviting Natalie to precede him. "Just follow the dog."

Smiling, she moved toward an open doorway that led into what she assumed was a family room. The dog was now in the arms of a little girl with bright red curls and a freckled, pixie face. She looked strikingly like her mother, who rose from the couch as Natalie came in.

"Natalie," Molly said, moving toward her. "We're so glad you could come tonight."

"I was delighted to be asked," Natalie fibbed politely.

Something made her glance behind her. Casey sat quietly in a rocking chair holding an infant and meeting Natalie's gaze with an openly amused expression that told her he knew she hadn't expected to see him there. "Hi, Natalie."

She managed to return the greeting casually enough. "Hello, Casey."

"Kyle and I haven't entertained since Micah was born, so we thought we'd turn this into a real dinner party," Molly explained cheerily. "We invited Jewel and Mack, but Jewel had her Bible study group tonight, and Mack said he was a little tired."

Natalie was on the verge of replying when something bumped her leg. She looked down to see Molly's three-year-old daughter tapping with one hand against Natalie's gray slacks in an obvious bid for attention. "Hi."

As an only child whose friends were mostly singles, Natalie had been around very few small children. She moistened her lips and said, "Hello, Olivia."

"This is Poppy," the child added, holding up the wriggling dog that seemed to be doing its best to lick every inch of Olivia's cheeks.

"Yes, Poppy and I met already."

"C'mon, Livvie, let's get you washed up for dinner," Kyle said, scooping up both daughter and dog. Natalie noticed his slight limp, but it didn't seem to impede his progress as he carried the giggling child and yipping dog out of the room.

Molly followed her family toward the door. "Make yourself comfortable, Natalie. I'll be ready to serve dinner in about five minutes."

"Let me help you," Natalie offered quickly.

But Molly shook her head. "Everything's almost ready. You stay and keep Casey company while he babysits for me."

Great. Casey and a baby. Both of whom made her unaccountably nervous.

She perched on the edge of an armchair, mentally groping for something to say. "How's your hand?"

He held his hand up, palm out, to show her a fresh bandage. "Much better. I'm keeping it covered just as a precaution, but I can tell it's going to heal quickly."

"That's good." That subject exhausted, she nodded toward the baby in the crook of Casey's arm. "You look pretty comfortable. Do you have a lot of experience with kids?"

Casey glanced down at the sleeping infant and chuckled. "In our family, it's hard to avoid them. I have fourteen first cousins on my dad's side—Molly's side—and several of them have kids. The Walker clan's pretty tight, always getting together for some occasion or another. It's not at all unusual for thirty or more of us to be gathered at the ranch that belongs to Molly's dad, my uncle, Jared."

Daunted by the mental image of all those relatives in one place, many of them children, she swallowed. "Wow."

Casey laughed, making the baby start a little, though he didn't wake up. "Yeah, a lot of people react that way."

"How many siblings do you have?"

He shook his head. "I'm an only. But I never lacked for playmates with so many cousins. Especially the twins, Andrew and Aaron. There's just a few months' difference between our ages and our fathers are identical twins, so we spent a lot of time together, along with our cousin Jason D'Alessandro, who's a couple years older than I am."

"Your father's a twin?"

"Right. And his brother has twin sons of his own. We're all used to seeing double."

"I see." Sounded a bit confusing to her, but then, she didn't have that much experience with family.

Her mother had a brother, but they hadn't lived in the same state for decades and didn't see each other very often, so Natalie hardly knew her cousins on that side. Her father had been one of four brothers. Jewel was the youngest sibling and the only girl. Because her father and Jewel had been the closest of the Lofton siblings, Natalie had seen her aunt Jewel more than the rest of the family. She'd always looked forward to summer vacations in Gatlinburg, back when her family had been intact and at least outwardly happy together.

Though he'd been a few years older than Natalie, Tommy had always been a gracious and patient host, taking his younger cousin hiking in the mountains, teaching her to fish in the numerous area streams and accompanying her to a nearby amusement park. He had even taken her white-water rafting when he was a mature eighteen and she a hero-worshipping fourteen-year-old.

She still missed Tommy with a pang like a knife through her heart whenever she remembered those happy childhood times, before her parents' divorce and before Tommy had joined the military. That had been one of the hardest things about coming here to lick her wounds and plan her future, knowing that she would be surrounded by memories of the cousin who'd been such a happy part of her past.

The baby in Casey's lap made a rather surprised sound and opened his eyes. He looked up to see who was holding him, then broke into a toothless grin.

"Well," Casey said, grinning back, "you wake up happy, don't you, tiger?"

Little Micah hooted as if in agreement.

Casey was still smiling when he glanced up at Natalie. "I've always had that effect on kids. They start laughing as soon as they see my face."

"You're very good with him," she repeated, unable to think of anything else to say.

Casey gave the babbling baby a couple of bounces, eliciting a shrill giggle. And then he glanced at her and startled her by asking, "You want to hold him?"

She quickly held up her hands in a backing-away gesture. "No, thank you. He looks quite happy where he is."

Casey lifted an eyebrow. "Don't you like kids?"

"Sure I do. As long as someone else is taking care of them."

Whatever Casey might have said in response was interrupted when Molly reappeared in the doorway. "Dinner is served, you two. Oh, the baby's awake. Here, Casey, I'll take him. You can show our guest of honor into the dining room."

Passing off the baby, Casey turned with a flourish to offer his arm to Natalie. "Looks like you're the guest of honor," he said lightly. "And I'm the designated escort. Madam?"

She hoped no one noticed her slight hesitation before she rested her hand lightly on his arm.

Chapter Three

It was an interesting evening, Natalie thought as the meal progressed. Though well-behaved for a preschooler, Olivia enjoyed attention and didn't mind performing for it. Kyle had to tell her a couple of times to settle down and eat, which worked for a few minutes until she thought of something else she wanted to say.

In contrast to her quiet husband, Molly was pretty much a nonstop talker. Not in a self-absorbed way, since she asked lots of questions and seemed genuinely interested in the replies. She just liked to keep the conversation lively.

Casey was charming. Articulate, amusing, quick-witted. Natalie couldn't help wondering why he was working as a less-than-proficient maintenance man. He seemed very fond of Molly, friendly with Kyle, indulgent with Olivia. He gave every appearance of being a happy young man without a care in the world. And yet...

There was something in his eyes. Something about the very

faint lines that appeared around his mouth on those rare occasions when she caught him not smiling. Maybe it was because she had her own secrets, but she had the distinct feeling that Casey's smiles and jokes were hiding something not so happy. She didn't know how he'd ended up working for his cousin's husband, but something told her he had a story as depressing as her own.

She didn't ask questions, partially because she didn't want to encourage him to ask questions in return. She had asked her aunt and uncle not to tell anyone why she'd left her job in Nashville. Molly and Kyle knew only that she was no longer affiliated with the firm and was taking some time off while making some inquiries toward a new position. She figured they knew there was more to it than that, but they respected her privacy.

No one mentioned careers during dinner, keeping the conversation focused on the children and on local events. They talked about the summer tourist season that had recently ended and the upcoming winter season which would bring in holiday travelers and snow skiers. Gatlinburg, Pigeon Forge and the surrounding towns were all decorating for Christmas, with light displays and special Christmas shows and attractions to entice visitors.

"Maybe you'll see some of the lights before you go back to Nashville," Molly said to Natalie while wiping blackberry cobbler from Olivia's chin.

"Maybe," Natalie said noncommittally, though holiday displays were pretty much the last thing on her mind right then. She wasn't in a holiday mood.

Though she consented to let Natalie help her clear the table after the meal, Molly refused to allow her to help clean the kitchen. "There's very little left to do. Kyle and I will take care of it together after we put the kids to bed."

Natalie lingered only a few minutes after the meal ended, just long enough that she hoped her visit wouldn't qualify as an eat-and-run. Her chance to escape appeared when Micah began to fuss and Molly explained that he was ready to be fed. Natalie excused herself then, thanking both Molly and Kyle for the nice meal and telling them she'd like to get back up the mountain before it got too late.

Casey stood when she did. "I'll walk you to your car."

"That isn't—"

But he'd already opened the door and was motioning for her to go out ahead of him. She stepped out, snuggling into her black leather coat when a cool night breeze swirled around her. Casey closed the door behind them then fell into step beside her. He hadn't donned a coat over the long-sleeve denim shirt he wore loose over a light gray T-shirt and jeans, but he didn't seem to notice the chill.

"Nice meal, wasn't it?"

She nodded. "Very."

"My cousin's quite a talker."

"I like her."

"Everyone does. She's a lot like her mom. My aunt Cassie."

"Cassie? Were you named after her?"

"No. Mine's a family name. On my mother's side." He pushed his hands into the pockets of his jeans. "I thought I'd come do some work on the outside of your cabin tomorrow, if that's okay with you."

"On a Saturday? Don't you take weekends off?"

He shrugged. "I don't really have anything else to do. And the weather's supposed to be nice tomorrow. In the sixties. Might as well take advantage of it."

Once again, she wondered about his background, and why he had nothing better to do on a nice Saturday than work on her cabin. But she simply said, "It doesn't matter to me if you come tomorrow. I'll be at my computer most of the day."

She suspected that he was as curious about her as she was about him, but he seemed no more willing to open the door to questions. He nodded. "So, I'll see you tomorrow then. I won't come too early, so you don't have to worry that I'll wake you at dawn hammering or anything."

"I tend to be an early riser anyway." She opened her car door. "Good night, Casey."

"Good night, Natalie. Drive carefully."

"Yes, I will. Thanks."

She noted in her rearview mirror that he waited until she'd started her car and exited the driveway before he turned to go back inside.

Natalie was in the living room with her laptop and a second cup of coffee when she heard Casey's truck in the driveway the next morning. He didn't come to the door to announce his arrival, probably because he knew she was expecting him to show up, but went straight to work on the outside repairs. She heard the hammering start and she hoped he didn't break anything today—especially any of his bones.

She sat on a deep-cushioned, comfortable, green micro-suede sofa facing a corner rock fireplace over which hung a flat-screen TV connected to a satellite dish on the roof. A DVD player, a selection of popular DVDs and a gaming system were discreetly hidden in a cabinet beside the fireplace. A recliner and a rocker were placed on either side of the couch, conve-nient for conversation, television or fire watching.

A wall of big windows and a sliding glass door that opened onto the deck were just beside the fireplace, providing scenic views of the surrounding mountaintops that could compete with any electronic media for entertainment value. From those windows, Natalie had watched birds, squirrels and deer emerging from the woods backed up to the small lawn area.

She tried to concentrate on her computer screen, but she had grimly decided that she was even worse at computer investigations than Casey was at maintenance work. She'd used every search engine she knew, but she'd found nothing about anyone in the firm that could be perceived as evidence that she'd been set up by one of them to take a professional fall.

So Cathy Linski had bought a new car. That was far from incontrovertible evidence of anything except possibly questionable financial judgment.

As for her P.I.—she was beginning to have some doubts about the guy. She had tried twice to reach him that morning, and had gotten nothing but his voice mail. She should have listened to her instincts when she'd first met him. A burly, former police officer in his late thirties, he'd seemed a little sleazy, a bit of a braggart and more than a little annoying. But she'd convinced herself that most private investigators were probably like that, and that she didn't have to like him personally to work with him. But had her intuition been trying to tell her that he wasn't going to be a reliable resource?

She set the computer aside in frustration, wondering what the hell she was supposed to do if neither her own clumsy research nor her P.I.'s efforts turned up the evidence she needed to clear her name. Try to believe that some other firm would take a chance and hire her on the basis of her word alone that she had not betrayed the attorney-client privilege for monetary gain? Open her own storefront practice and pray the scandal wasn't uncovered to humiliate her? Give up and find another career despite the long years of training she had put in to establish this one?

A tap on the back door broke into her unhappy musings. Sighing, she walked into the kitchen, hoping the first aid kit had the supplies to handle whatever Casey's latest crisis was.

Automatically running a hand through her hair, she opened the door. "Good morning."

Looking as good as ever, maybe even a little better since he wore a dark green, long-sleeve T-shirt that really brought out the emerald in his multicolored eyes, Casey smiled. "Morning. Hope I'm not bothering you."

She shook her head, thinking he couldn't know how relieved she was to be sidetracked from what she'd been doing. "You aren't."

"Do you have an old bowl or pot or something I can put some food in? There's a stray dog out here that looks pretty hungry."

Despite not being a "dog person," Natalie didn't like the thought of any creature suffering. "Hold on. I'll find something."

He was looking over his shoulder, presumably at the stray. "Okay, thanks. If you have any scraps or leftovers—"

"I'll look."

It took her only a couple of minutes to unearth an empty plastic margarine tub from one of the cabinets and fill it with water. She pulled a plate of leftover meat loaf from the fridge, nuked it just long enough to soften it, and carried both food and water to Casey. "Here. Give him this."

Casey studied the meat loaf warily. "Are there onions in this? Because onions are really bad for dogs."

"They're bad for me, too," she replied with a shake of her head. "They give me headaches. No onion in the meat loaf. Just meat, egg, ketchup, a little bell pepper and a little mustard."

"Sounds safe enough in the absence of real dog food. Better than starving, anyway."

Mildly curious, and needing a distraction from her frustration, she followed him outside to get a look at the stray he'd found. She didn't bother to grab a jacket. The air was cool, but the thin red sweater she wore with her jeans was sufficient. If she happened to notice that Casey looked darned good in his own jeans from behind, she didn't let herself dwell on the view. She forced herself to search for the dog instead.

It was a medium-sized mutt, probably a mottled brown and white after a bath, but mostly brown now. Its hair was matted, and Natalie could almost count its ribs. The dog didn't run when Casey walked slowly toward it, but neither did it allow him to get too close, slinking backward as Casey neared. Casey stopped and set the food and water on the ground, then backed away without making any sudden moves.

"There you go, buddy. It's all yours," he said in a low, almost crooning voice. "We're going to stay way back here and let you have all you want."

The dog's nose twitched as the aroma of the hastily warmed meat loaf reached it. Head lowered, wary eyes still fixed on the watching humans, it took a couple of tentative steps forward and sniffed the food. Moments later the plate was empty and the dog was noisily lapping up water to wash down its meal.

Watching sympathetically, Natalie asked, "Should we call animal control?"

She knew very well that the dog didn't understand her, but the minute she'd finished speaking, it turned and ran into the woods, disappearing into the trees and undergrowth.

Casey looked at her and shrugged. "I don't see any point now. By the time someone got here, that dog could be anywhere. At least he's had a good meal today."

"Was it a male?"

He shrugged again. "I have no idea."

"Oh." Hoping the dog would find another good meal soon,

she gathered the empty plate and the half-empty bowl of water to take back inside. She turned to look at the ladder propped against the cabin and an open toolbox on the ground beside it. "How's the work going today?"

Casey pushed a hand through his hair. "Okay. I've been cleaning the gutters, mostly. Hammered out a couple of dents to let the water flow better. I noticed some shingles that need to be replaced, but I'll have to have help with that, since I've never done roofing. And I've still got to caulk and do some winterizing before the really cold weather sets in. Clean and waterproof the deck. And then Kyle and I are going to install the hot tub."

"Hot tub?"

His lips twitched. "Yeah. It's going onto the far end of the deck. Kyle said it seems like everyone wants a hot tub with their cabins these days. A lot of the cabins around here have pool tables and arcade-style video game rooms, but they want to keep this one a little more rustic."

"Oh, I agree," she said, glancing at the tidy little cabin that had offered her such welcome seclusion these past few days. She supposed a hot tub on the deck wouldn't be so bad, for vacationers who liked to soak away tension while they relaxed, but the cabin really needed nothing more. There were hiking trails nearby, a rushing stream that passed right alongside the edge of the property, bird baths and feeders, a grill and picnic table, swings and rockers and chairs on the front porch and back deck for sitting and admiring the spectacular view. Who would want to play video games when they had all of nature for a playground?

Not that she'd taken full advantage of those pleasures while she'd been here. She'd been so obsessed with her problems. She would make a point to sit out on the deck that very day, she promised herself, even if it was with her computer.

"I guess I'd better get back to work," Casey said, turning

toward the house. "I'm going to start on the deck after I finish cleaning that last gutter. You weren't planning to use the deck today, were you?"

Mentally revising the plans she had just made, she shook her head. "Not if you need to work on it."

"Winter's going to be here before we know it and the maintenance work is sort of behind because of the regular handyman's accident. I told Kyle I'd get as much done as I can today while he works on one of the other rentals."

"Of course. I'll let you get back to work."

"Thanks for helping with the dog."

She nodded and moved toward the house. An odd feeling hit her as she walked out of the sunny, pleasantly cool daylight and into the almost hauntingly empty cabin. It wasn't exactly dark inside, since the cabin was well-lit and had plenty of windows to let in the sunlight and the mountain views. But it somehow felt dim and lonely to her as her eyes were drawn to the computer sitting on the coffee table, animated fish swimming lifelessly across the screen.

Setting the bowl and plate in the sink, she crossed her arms over her chest, chilled now in a way she hadn't been while out in the sun with Casey.

An hour later, Casey was moving furniture off the deck when the back door opened and Natalie stepped out. She carried an insulated, stainless-steel mug and her expression was oddly guarded. Almost as if she were nervous about something.

"I made a fresh pot of coffee," she said when he turned to look at her. "Would you like a cup?"

He had just opened a bottle of water, but he could drink that later. "Sure," he said, pleased that she'd made the gesture. "That sounds good, thanks."

She handed him the mug, then glanced around the deck, from which he'd already removed the Adirondack chairs and the matching end table that sat between them. He still had to move a wrought-iron umbrella table and the four iron spring chairs surrounding it, and a couple of large planters that sat on wrought iron bases to protect the decking. A wooden swing hung on chains at the far end of the deck. That, too, would need a coat of waterproofing sealant.

"Where are you putting the furniture?"

Carefully swallowing a sip of the hot coffee, he lowered the mug to answer. "At the end of the cabin, on the concrete slab with the grill and the picnic table."

"Could you use some help moving the rest of it? I'd like to do something useful since Aunt Jewel and Uncle Mack have been so generous letting me stay here."

He made an effort to hide his surprise. "I won't turn down an offer to help. But you're sure there isn't something you'd rather be doing? It's such a beautiful day."

She glanced around as if she'd barely noticed. "I have nothing else to do," she said.

Just the hint of dejection in her voice made his heart soften. What was it about Natalie Lofton that reminded him a little bit of the stray dog they had just fed? Isolated, wary, maybe mistreated at some point, but still with an undeniable air of quiet dignity?

Suspecting that she wouldn't appreciate that analogy at all— would more likely hate it, in fact—he kept it to himself. Setting the coffee mug on the wide deck railing, he nodded toward the wrought iron dining set. "We can start moving the chairs."

She turned in that direction. Casey reached out to detain her. "Do you have a pair of work gloves?" he asked, glancing down at her soft-looking hands. "You don't want to risk blisters."

"I have driving gloves. And some knit gloves designed for warmth."

"Either would be better than nothing."

"Then I'll be right back. Is there anything else we need from inside?"

"No." He took hold of the first chair. "I'll take this one down."

He was returning from that short trip when he met up with Natalie again. Her hands protected by leather driving gloves, she lugged one of the chairs, hindered more by its awkward shape than by weight. He almost offered to help her, but something about the way she looked at him warned him that she'd rather do it herself.

He both understood and respected pride. Nodding, he moved past her to get the third chair. They would carry the table together, he decided. To be honest, he wasn't sure how he'd have gotten it down the steps by himself. But because of his own slightly overdeveloped ego, he probably wouldn't have asked for her help had she not offered.

They worked together for the next two hours, removing the remainder of the furnishings and then cleaning the deck with brooms and a small power washer Casey had brought with him. They didn't talk much, but the quiet was companionable. The sounds of singing birds and rushing water and dried leaves blowing across the ground provided a sound track for their efforts.

Though he didn't allow himself to stare openly at her, Casey observed Natalie surreptitiously as she worked. He was pleased to see a tint of color in her cheeks, a new sparkle of accomplishment in her eyes. She liked having a purpose, he decided, something that made her feel useful. And the crisp, fresh air wasn't hurting either, since she'd been spending entirely too much time holed up in the cabin, from what he had observed.

"That looks good," he announced a short while later as he

and Natalie stood back to admire their work. "Tomorrow morning I'll apply the sealer. We can replace the furniture in twenty-four to forty-eight hours after that, according to the instructions on the can."

"There's a lot of maintenance involved with these cabins, isn't there? It's mind-boggling how much hard work is involved in being a vacation landlord."

"Yeah. Kyle and Mack both put in long days, especially now that their full-time maintenance guy's on the bench. And your aunt stays busy with the books and reservations."

Still looking at the empty deck, Natalie murmured, "Tommy used to complain that his family lived in a vacation destination and never had time to actually take a holiday\themselves. I didn't understand when I was a kid, but I certainly do now."

Casey studied her face, regretting that he saw shadows of sadness in her eyes again. "Kyle's talked about your cousin. It sounds as if he was a great guy."

"He was."

Seeing movement out of the corner of his eye, he turned, thinking maybe the stray dog had come back for dinner. Instead, he saw a small herd of deer wander out of the woods, grazing on the grass of the lawn. He counted three full-grown does and another that might have been a young buck.

"Natalie," he said softly, nodding in that direction. "Look."

She turned her head, then smiled. "They're beautiful."

"They are, aren't they?"

They watched in silence for a moment, and then something—a scent, a motion, a sound, perhaps—startled one of the does. She lifted her head, looked directly at Casey and Natalie, and then turned to melt back into the woods, followed by her companions.

"We've certainly seen the animals today, haven't we?" Natalie said, looking at him again. "Think a black bear will come out of the woods next?"

He grinned. "I kind of hope not. Dogs and deer I can handle. Bears—not so much."

She chuckled. "The ones around here usually leave you alone if you do the same with them. Tommy and I saw one on a hike once. It looked at us, we looked at it, and then we all turned and went our own ways. Fortunately, Tommy and I had been making a lot of noise, so we didn't startle the bear when we appeared. That's when they're particularly dangerous, when they're frightened or protecting their young."

"We didn't see many bears back in Dallas. Saw a few rattlesnakes on my uncle's ranch. I didn't care for them, either."

Natalie shuddered delicately. "Neither would I. I don't like snakes."

"Ah. So there is something that intimidates the intrepid Natalie Lofton."

"Intrepid?" she repeated, lifting an eyebrow.

Shrugging, he admitted, "It's a word I tend to associate with you, for some reason. Maybe because you seem so hard to rattle. Broken pipes, blood, stray dogs—bears, apparently. You deal with it all without blinking. I've only heard you admit to two things that intimidate you—snakes and babies."

She blinked and he could tell that he had taken her completely off-guard, something that apparently didn't happen much with her. And then she gave a little smile that didn't quite reach her somber eyes and said, "I'll admit to being wary of both snakes and babies, though maybe not quite to the same extent. As for the rest—I'm not sure *intrepid* is the word to describe me. Trust me, I don't handle everything as calmly as you suggest."

"Coulda fooled me."

He'd always considered himself fairly proficient in interpreting body language. Something about the way she crossed her arms and then huddled a bit into her sweater made him wonder what it meant. A slightly self-protective gesture, perhaps hinting at a recent blow that had been difficult for her to handle? Or was she just chilly and he was reading too much into the emotions he'd thought he glimpsed in her expression?

"The temperature seems to be dropping," he commented, telling himself to mind his own business. "Maybe you'd better go back inside."

She glanced again at the clean, empty deck. "I guess so, since we're finished here. You're done for the day, aren't you?"

"Yeah. It's getting too close to dark to start anything else. I guess I'll head on back to the cabin I'm staying in. I'm going to do some work on the floors there this evening. I'm sanding and refinishing them, starting in the kitchen."

"So you're working on both at once?"

"Pretty much. The regular maintenance guy had already finished the outside of mine before he was in the accident. So I've been working inside there for a couple hours a day after leaving here."

"I know Kyle and Uncle Mack must appreciate your help."

He shrugged. "As you're well aware, I'm not the most skilled handyman, but I want to contribute what I can while I'm here."

She took a step toward the cabin, then stopped and looked back at him. He could almost see a debate going on in her head before she asked, "You said you're working on the kitchen floor in your cabin?"

"Yeah. I've got the room cleaned out and everything taped off, so I'm going to start sanding tonight."

"What about dinner?"

"I figured I'd pick up a burger and fries on the way."

She took a quick deep breath and then said very casually, "I have a few things I can make quickly here if you'd like to eat with me before you go. If you're going to put in more hours of work this evening, you need to eat something a little more nutritious than a burger and fries."

Though he was surprised that she'd offered, Casey didn't hesitate to accept. "I'd love to join you for dinner. Thanks."

She smiled somewhat tentatively. "Okay. Great. Come on in and you can wash up while I get started."

Leaving his toolbox at the foot of the steps, he followed close behind her as she moved toward the door.

Chapter Four

Casey entered the kitchen a short time later sniffing the air. "Something smells really good."

Her hands protected by oven mitts, she set the pan of broiled fish on a trivet. "I hope you like fish tacos."

"Love 'em."

They sat at the kitchen table with their meals, and Natalie searched her mind for conversational topics that didn't stray too far into personal territory. They talked more about the renovations to the cabin, and a few more things that needed to be done inside before it was rented out again. They chatted about the A-frame in which Casey had been staying, and how Kyle and Mack had decided to install a pool table in the loft now being used as a cozy sitting room with a spectacular view.

Casey admitted he hadn't taken advantage of the many local tourist attractions during his stay. He added that Molly wanted him to accompany her and Olivia to the Dollywood theme park the following week, leaving the baby with Jewel. Kyle wasn't enthusiastic about amusement parks, but Molly had promised Olivia she would take her soon.

"I haven't been to the park in years," Natalie said, "but I always had a good time there. I'm sure you'll have fun with Molly and Olivia."

Casey took another bite of his almost completely eaten taco. Washing it down with a sip of the peach tea she had prepared, he complimented her again on the simple meal. That led to a casual discussion of their favorite foods and specialty restaurants.

"There's a place back home in Dallas that makes the best barbecue pizza anywhere," Casey enthused. "Topped with pulled pork, barbecue sauce, onions, jalapeños and three different kinds of cheese. The best."

"Sounds messy."

"Totally. And a lot of people follow it up with an antacid chaser. But it's still good."

"I've only been to Texas a few times," she said. "And then only to Dallas and Houston for business purposes. I haven't seen much of the state except for the insides of some very nice conference hotels."

"Oh, there's lots to see in Texas," he assured her. "From the coast to the plains, it's a pretty diverse state. I've spent most of my life in the Dallas area."

"I always seem to be there midsummer. It was always hot."

He shrugged. "You get used to it."

"Will you be going back soon?"

She hadn't meant to ask any questions for fear of giving him an opening to ask a few in return. That one had just slipped out.

Casey didn't seem to find the offhand inquiry particularly significant. "Yeah. I guess. I mean, well, most of my family's there. I just came here to visit Molly and Kyle, and then I volunteered to help out a little with the repairs. I'll probably head back to Texas in another week or so."

She couldn't help noticing that he looked as if he were discussing an upcoming dental procedure. What was so bad at home that he would rather hole up here, cleaning gutters and scrubbing a deck on a pleasant Saturday?

He gave a slight shake of his head, as if clearing his mind of unpleasant thoughts. "What about you? When are you going back to Nashville?"

"I don't know yet," she said, looking down at her plate. "I'm...between jobs at the moment, and I'm taking the time to make some career decisions."

She stood abruptly before he could respond. "Aunt Jewel made me one of her famous key lime pies. I haven't even had a chance to cut into it yet. Would you like a slice for dessert?"

"Sure. I love key lime pie."

"I'll make some decaf coffee to go with it."

"Anything I can do to help?"

"No, thanks. It'll just take a few minutes. Feel free to move into the living room, if you'd be more comfortable. The TV remote is on the coffee table if you want to watch the news or something while I make the coffee."

"Yeah, I think I'll check the weather forecasts. I'm hoping they aren't predicting rain tomorrow. I'd like to get the sealant applied to the deck in the morning."

"Sure, go ahead. I'll bring the pie and coffee into the living room when it's ready."

She heard a weatherman's booming voice from the other room before she even had the kettle filled with water. Setting the kettle on a burner, she scooped coffee beans into the small grinder she'd brought with her from home.

It had been surprisingly easy to be with Casey tonight, she

mused as she transferred the coarsely ground coffee into a French press and set a kitchen timer for four minutes. He hadn't done anything to make her feel uncomfortable, hadn't asked any questions except a follow-up to the one she'd asked. He'd been pleasant, entertaining, a little flirtatious. And her bruised feminine ego had responded eagerly.

She needed this right now, she told herself. Needed to spend some time with someone who wasn't looking at her suspiciously, who could make her forget about all the problems back home and just have a little fun for a change.

She was in no hurry for the evening to end.

Casey sprawled on the couch, a remote in his hand as he only half concentrated on the cable weather channel playing on the flat-screen TV above the fireplace. He jumped to his feet when Natalie appeared around the partial wall that separated the kitchen from the living room. He cleared off a couple of books and a basket of apples from the coffee table so she could set the tray there.

"Wow, that pie looks good," he said as Natalie took a seat on the couch beside him. He noted that she could have sat in one of the chairs, but she'd chosen to sit next to him instead. Very friendly and companionable. Maybe she was starting to like him a little despite his questionable maintenance skills.

Unaware of the direction his thoughts were taking, she replied lightly to his comment, "My aunt is a really good cook. Desserts are her specialty."

"It tastes even better than it looks," he said, swallowing a creamy bite and reaching for his coffee. "Good coffee, too," he said after taking a cautious sip of the hot beverage.

"Thanks. I buy my beans from a coffee and tea specialty store in Nashville. It's one of my favorite places to browse."

He set his cup down and then turned to face her on the couch while he swallowed another bite of the pie. He was fully aware that she didn't want to answer questions about herself. He'd have to be blind to miss the signals. While she was perfectly amenable to congenial small talk, she had no intention of sharing too much of herself.

He'd gone along with her obvious wishes during dinner. But now he was tempted to push his luck a little. Because Natalie Lofton intrigued him too much for him not to at least try to learn a little more about her. Preferably from her, rather than anyone else.

"How long have you lived in Nashville?" That seemed an innocuous enough way to begin.

She looked into her coffee cup. "Pretty much all my life."

"I've always lived within a few miles of Dallas, myself," he confided. "I guess we have that in common. Not moving around a lot, I mean."

"I suppose so."

He suspected that she did not want to talk about careers, since she didn't seem to have one at the moment. He wasn't particularly interested in talking about his own, either. He would be hard-pressed to explain exactly what had led him to take an unpaid and inconveniently timed leave of absence.

Family seemed like another relatively harmless topic. "Do your parents still live in Nashville?"

"No. My mother and her husband live in Mississippi, and my dad lives in London."

He hadn't realized that her parents were divorced. He knew his family was atypical, but divorce just didn't happen in the Walker clan, so it hadn't occurred to him. But she hadn't sounded particularly bitter, so maybe that wasn't a sensitive subject for her. "Your dad is Jewel's brother, right?"

"Yes. They were the closest in age of the five siblings."

"Five?"

She nodded. "Only three are still living."

"So you come from a big family, too."

"You'd think so, but Tommy was Aunt Jewel's only son, I'm Dad's only offspring, one of my uncles never had children and the others had three kids between them, none of whom I know very well. I asked my dad once why his family wasn't closer and he said he didn't really know. They just drifted apart after their mother died when he and Aunt Jewel were still in school."

"But you've been close to your aunt."

"Yes. Not as close as I would have liked, since we live several hours apart, and I haven't been able to make it to east Tennessee very often the last few years. But we've always had a special bond between us."

"I'm pretty close to my aunts, too," he offered. "Especially Aunt Taylor—she's married to my dad's twin brother. Since I was almost always with their boys, Aaron and Andrew, she and my mom claim they pretty much co-mothered the three of us. The rest of the family called us the 'terrible trio.'"

That made her laugh, and he found himself mesmerized by a quick flash of dimples at the corners of her mouth. He hadn't noticed those before—but he hadn't seen her laugh that many times before. At the risk of sounding clichéd, he thought she really should do so more often.

"I don't know why that doesn't surprise me," she said. "Were you known as, um, accident-prone, perhaps?"

He frowned at her. "Very funny."

"Sorry." She set her empty pie plate back on the tray. "You said you and your twin cousins are the same age?"

"Almost. Aaron and Andrew are a few months younger than I am. They're twenty-five. I turned twenty-six in July."

She gave a little smile. "I'll celebrate my thirtieth birthday this coming January."

Which confirmed his guess about her age. "So you're, what? An Aquarius?"

She waved a hand. "Capricorn, though I don't really follow horoscopes."

"I'm a Leo. I have a cousin who's recently gotten into that sort of thing. She's pretty good with it. It's amazing how accurate she can be with her charting and stuff."

His cousin Dawne had actually warned him that he was headed for a crisis a year ago, when it had appeared to everyone else—and to him, for that matter—that he was leading a charmed life. She'd seen something in his stars that had told her he had some serious choices to make, and that the outcome of those choices could lead either to a lifetime of contentment or one of quiet despair.

He'd almost forgotten that conversation until now. Maybe he should call Dawne tomorrow and ask if her star charts had any useful advice for him now that he'd actually reached the crossroads he'd been warned about.

Natalie seemed to have no interest in discussing astrology. "Can I get you any more coffee?"

"No, thanks. I guess I'd better be leaving if I'm going to get more done tonight."

She put her cup on the tray. "Just set your dishes on the tray," she said, motioning toward the coffee cup he'd just drained. "I'll take care of them."

Somewhat reluctantly, he stood. "Thanks for the meal, Natalie. It was really good."

She walked with him toward the door. "It was nice having the company." She sounded as if she really meant it.

"So I'll see you tomorrow then. I should be around sometime late morning to waterproof the deck."

"I won't be here much tomorrow. I promised Aunt Jewel I'd join them for church in the morning and then for Sunday lunch. Do you have a key if you need to get into the cabin while I'm gone?"

He told himself there was no reason for him to be disappointed that she had other plans. He wasn't coming back for social reasons, but to work. He probably wouldn't have seen her much, anyway. "I'll bring Kyle's key, but I'm planning on just working outside tomorrow."

"Yes, well, feel free to come in if you need anything."

"Thanks." He stepped out onto the porch, then hesitated. Turning, he said, "Hey, Natalie?"

She paused in the act of closing the door behind him. "Yes?"

"Maybe I could return the favor sometime. Treat you to dinner, I mean." Not exactly a smooth invitation, he thought with a slight wince. "There's a really nice steak-and-seafood place in town. I've been told the trout there is the best. Maybe we could try it out one night this week?"

He could almost see the debate going on inside her head. She looked tempted…but a little nervous about accepting. What was it about him that would make her nervous?

"Maybe," she said after a moment. "If there's time."

He wasn't sure what that meant, but at least it wasn't an outright rejection. "Okay. We'll talk about it later then."

She moved back a step into the cabin. "Good night, Casey."

"Goo—"

But she had already closed the door between them.

Casey's truck was in the driveway when Natalie returned to the cabin after visiting her aunt and uncle for most of Sunday afternoon. The fact that her heart started beating a little faster at the thought of seeing him again made her pause behind the wheel.

She winced as she remembered her reaction when he'd asked her out. Even though he'd framed the invitation as a way of repaying her for the dinner, it had been clear that what he'd suggested was a date. She'd been so disconcerted that she'd all but shut the door in his face. It wasn't like her to be so flustered by a simple dinner invitation.

The truth was, Casey Walker made her nervous. And while she'd told herself that it was nice to have such an attractive diversion from her current problems, she wondered if it would be a mistake to get involved—even temporarily—with a good-looking, younger man who obviously harbored secrets of his own.

She really should be focusing more intently on her problems at home, she chided herself. She didn't have time for a dalliance. But Casey was pure temptation in blue jeans and a tool belt. Would there really be any harm in flirting with him a bit while Beecham conducted her investigation?

Carrying the bag of leftovers her aunt had insisted on sending with her, she entered through the front door and went straight to the kitchen to put the food away. She debated whether she should go out to greet Casey. It wasn't as if he was there for a social reason. He was working, and she didn't want to interfere with that process.

Coward.

She slammed the refrigerator door shut, annoyed with that nagging little voice in her head and with herself for acting so foolishly. And then she cursed herself again when someone knocked loudly on the front door and she almost jumped out of her shoes.

Sighing in exasperation, she walked through the living room to open the front door with a smile. "Hello, Casey."

He nodded, looking a little distracted. He wore a denim shirt, blue plaid flannel jacket and jeans, all of which showed evidence that he'd been doing rather dirty manual labor that day. "Hi. Listen, that dog's hovering around again. I think maybe he came back for another meal. Do you have anything?"

"I just brought home enough leftover pot roast for a whole pack of dogs. I'll get him some, and a bowl of water."

"I'll come in and help you carry it out. We can't walk on the deck because the sealant is still drying."

"All right."

He followed her into the kitchen. "Did you have a nice visit with your aunt and uncle?"

She answered as she refilled the plastic bowl she'd used the day before with fresh water. "Yes, I did. Very nice."

Handing him the water, she opened the fridge and pulled out the plate of leftover roast. "Did you have any problems sealing the deck?" she asked to keep the small talk going.

"No. I used Kyle's sprayer and everything worked fine."

"Good. So I should be able to walk on it tomorrow?"

"Yeah. Give it twenty-four hours or so and it should be good to go."

She warmed the meat just to room temperature, only a few seconds. She didn't want the hungry dog to burn its mouth. "Okay," she said, taking the plate from the microwave. "Let's go see if he's still there."

"I have a feeling he will be," Casey replied, letting her precede him. "He looked pretty hungry. And hopeful."

"Should we call animal control while it's here?"

Casey hesitated. "Give me a couple of days to see if I can make friends with him first. Maybe Kyle will know someone who'd give the dog a home if we can get it to trust us."

Natalie was still wearing the clothes she had donned for

church that morning, a black waist-length jacket buttoned over a lace-trimmed green cami with a knee-length, black-and-green checked skirt. Fortunately, her black shoes had a reasonably sensible, two-inch heel so she had little trouble following Casey across the uneven lawn toward the woods.

She spotted the dog just as Casey stopped ahead of her. Looking as ragged and dirty as it had the day before, it lurked in the shadows, watching them warily, prepared to run if they made any sudden moves.

Holding the water bowl in his left hand, Casey reached out with his right to take the food plate from Natalie. He crooned quietly to the dog as he took a few slow steps forward and knelt to set the bowls on the ground. "Here you go, buddy. Come on. Have some nice pot roast."

Casey stayed by the plates, waiting to see if the dog was hungry enough to approach the food even with Casey so close. The dog remained where it was, looking from the food to Casey and then back again, its thin body quivering.

Casey sighed, stood and moved back to Natalie's side, several yards from the food. "Okay. We won't get too close."

Apparently reassured, the dog crept closer to the food. It ate quickly, finishing the roast and then cleaning the plate with a few more licks before washing the meal down with several noisy laps of water. Satisfied, it looked at Natalie and Casey again. After a moment in which none of them moved, it gave a couple of quick, tentative wags of its matted tail, then turned and ran back into the woods.

"I think he thanked us," Casey murmured, glancing at Natalie with a grin.

Though she wasn't prone to anthropomorphizing, she returned the smile and said, "Maybe he did. Do you think he'll be back?"

"Could be. I'll pick up some dog food this evening. That would be healthier for him than table scraps."

"I'm not sure we're doing him any favors by not calling animal control. At least he'd be safe and well-fed in an animal shelter. And the nights are starting to get pretty cold."

"I don't think they'd be able to catch him," Casey argued. "And I don't like the thought of him being trapped. I think I'll be able to tame him enough to find him a home. He seems like he wants to make friends. He's just a little skittish."

"And how long do you think it will take to tame him to that point?"

"I, uh, don't know," he admitted with a shrug. "If I haven't made any progress in the next couple of days, I'll call animal control and ask for advice."

She looked at him curiously. "Why are you so reluctant to call them? I'm sure they can catch him very humanely. And it would be so much safer for him to be…"

"In a cage?" Casey broke in to ask. "Deprived of his freedom and locked up somewhere for his own good?"

Startled by his tone, she tilted her head to study him more closely. "Um—?"

His face darkened with what might have been a flush. "Sorry. You're right, he'd probably be better off in a shelter. But I'd still like to give it a couple of days. The weather's supposed to be nice for the rest of the week, so I think he'll be fine."

She couldn't say she understood, but it wasn't as if the dog was bothering her. "Should we leave the water bowl out?"

Still looking a little sheepish, Casey shrugged. "Wouldn't hurt, though there's plenty of water around this area."

"And the food?"

"No. Too many other critters to be lured out if you leave food sitting out here. We'll just feed the dog when we see him."

She nodded and picked up the empty plate. "Fine. There's more of the leftover pot roast, if you're hungry."

He chuckled. "Feeding the other stray in your yard?"

Smiling a little, she said, "I'll even get you a bowl of water, if you're thirsty."

He shook his head. "Thanks, but I've already eaten. I brought lunch with me today. I ate at the picnic table and enjoyed the view. It was nice."

"So, you're finished for the day?"

"Almost. I just need to do a little more caulking on the west end of the cabin. Maybe another hour or so today."

She nodded. "Let me know if you need anything. I'll be inside."

"Okay, thanks."

Without looking back at him, she went inside. She changed into jeans and a sweater, then put water on to boil for tea. Her computer sat on the coffee table. She reached for it, then changed her mind. She just couldn't face another fruitless search right then.

Glancing at her watch, she noted that it was only four o'clock. She had a long evening ahead with little to do. It was too late to go out for a walk, since it would be dark soon. She thought about calling someone—her mom, her dad, or Amber, maybe. But she couldn't think of anything to say if she did. Nothing had changed.

She picked up a novel she'd been trying to read for the past week, though she'd had a hard time concentrating on it. She made it through about five pages before a tap on the front door brought her attention out of the story again.

The way Casey glanced downward let her know he'd noticed she'd changed clothes, though he didn't comment. "I'm calling it a day. Anything you need before I leave?"

"No, thank you. Have a nice evening."

His mouth crooked into a wry smile in response to her ridiculously clichéd words. "Thanks. Same to you."

She'd almost closed the door before she jerked it impulsively back open. "Casey?"

Halfway down the steps, he looked over his shoulder. "Yeah?"

She tried to think of a good reason to keep him there a little longer, to delay the inevitable return to solitude and worry. "Do you like to play games? You know, cards and board games?"

His eyes lit up. "Sure. Doesn't everyone?"

"I found a whole stack of games in the cabinet next to the fireplace. Maybe you'd like to stay and play Scrabble or something for a while? I have some of Aunt Jewel's leftovers I can heat for dinner. If you don't have any other plans, of course," she finished, belatedly realizing that he might have things he'd rather do.

He smiled. "I was going to work in the cabin tonight, but playing games sounds like a much nicer way to spend the evening. I warn you, though, I'm pretty good at Scrabble. And I play to win."

Something about his smile made her very glad she'd let herself give in to temptation. She smiled back at him, ignoring the little voice in her head warning her to step carefully. "So do I."

He walked back up the steps. "Looks like the competition's on."

Chapter Five

Casey could almost see Natalie loosening up as the evening progressed. She had been so tense earlier, her eyes shadowed, her mouth taut, but after a couple of no-holds-barred Scrabble games, one game won by each of them, she was laughing and relaxed. He took full credit for the transformation, though he did so privately.

"Would you like another glass of wine?" she asked, reaching for the bottle on the table beside her glass.

Okay, so maybe he couldn't take all the credit, he thought, shaking his head with a smile. "I have to drive in a little while. Considering those winding roads, I'd better stick to coffee now."

She slapped her forehead lightly. "Of course. I wasn't even thinking. Let me refill your coffee cup."

"Thanks."

She poured herself another glass of white wine. "Whose turn is it?"

"Yours." He tapped the Scrabble board. "I played 'quid.' For a tidy number of points, I might add, considering that the Q is on a triple-letter square."

She studied his play and then her tiles. A smile tipped up her lips, and then she set several tiles on the board with a flourish. "Vista," she said rather gloatingly. "With, you will note, the S in front of your 'quid,' turning it into 'squid.' And may I also direct your attention to the triple-*word* square beneath the V."

He couldn't help laughing at her obvious delight in besting him. As competitive as he was, he didn't mind losing when Natalie seemed to be having such a nice time winning. Whether because of the wine or the game or—he wanted to believe—the company, she was smiling more than he'd ever seen her, and the lighthearted mood looked good on her.

"It's been years since I played board games," she said, taking another sip of the wine. "I'd almost forgotten how much fun they can be."

He picked up his coffee mug. "Your friends back in Nashville don't get together to play games?"

Her smile dimmed a few watts. "Not so much. I've been hanging around with a bunch of workaholics for the past few years, I guess. Their idea of fun is a cocktail party with plenty of networking opportunities."

So she'd been corporate. Didn't surprise him. He still couldn't decide if she'd burned out or lost her job, but something made him suspect the latter. Laying out tiles to spell "maid," the longest word he could manage at the time, he said casually, "Sounds to me like you needed a vacation."

"I suppose I did." She took a few moments to study her tile rack, then played on his M.

"Not much fun, though, if you're spending it all here in this cabin."

She shrugged. "I needed the rest."

"Maybe you'd like to do something a little different this week? Maybe a hike or something? I've been told there are some pretty nice trails around here."

"I haven't been hiking in a long time, either. But maybe I will go this week."

"You know, this is my first visit to this area. I'd like to go with you on a hike, if you don't mind."

She didn't even hesitate this time before she picked up her wine glass again and nodded. "Sure. Why not? I could use the diversion."

He wasn't sure how he felt about being used as a diversion—but then again, wasn't that what he was looking for, as well? Something to think about other than returning home and taking up his life where he'd left off—a prospect that left him feeling empty and inexplicably anxious?

She won the game, by less than twenty points. "That makes you the champ tonight," he said. "Two games to one."

"It was close," she replied, beginning to gather the game pieces. "We're pretty evenly matched."

He thought about those words for a moment, but decided not to comment on them. Instead, he took another sip of coffee while Natalie closed the Scrabble game box.

Her gaze met his across the table between them and he was struck by something he saw in her eyes. His well-developed intuition told him that though she had laughed and played for a couple of hours, something was still eating at her. Something an evening of games—and half a bottle of wine—couldn't entirely banish.

He wondered just how much of a "diversion" she was looking for with him.

She drained the wine from her glass, and looked for a

moment as if she were tempted to refill it again. But then she pushed her glass away and replaced the stopper in the wine bottle. "Can I get you some more coffee?"

"Actually, it's getting late. I guess I'd better be going."

He saw the expression in her eyes before she lowered her lids, but he couldn't interpret what he had seen. Was she reluctant for him to leave? If so, was it because she really wanted him to stay—or because she didn't want to be alone?

She followed him through the living room. "I'll see you tomorrow, I suppose."

"Yeah. Thanks for dinner. And the games."

"You're welcome. I enjoyed the company."

"You mean, the diversion," he murmured, remembering what she'd said earlier.

"That, too," she replied with a slight shrug.

She reached for the door at the same time he did. They collided, and Casey caught her shoulders to steady her. "Okay?"

Smiling a bit sheepishly up at him, she said, "Clumsy. I rarely drink wine. I must have overdone it a little tonight."

He didn't release her immediately. Nor did she step away, instead gazing up at him as he searched her face. Her cheeks were a bit flushed, her eyes a little too bright, and it was all he could do not to cover her slightly parted lips with his own. He suspected she knew full well that he wanted to kiss her. Just as he suspected she wouldn't mind so much. Maybe she even wanted him to kiss her.

But because she'd had too much wine, and because she'd admitted that she wasn't quite steady tonight, he allowed himself only to touch her face as he brushed back a strand of hair from her cheek.

He wanted to tell her that he was a pretty good listener, if she wanted to talk, but he didn't think she would respond to that just now. It was obvious that she didn't want to talk about whatever had brought her here, which he could certainly understand. But he wanted to do something to make her feel better.

"I was serious about wanting to go on a hike with you," he said, keeping his tone casual. "It sounds like fun. How about tomorrow morning? I can't put the furniture back on the deck until afternoon at the earliest, so I don't have a lot to do tomorrow. Unless *you* have something you would rather do?"

Her mouth twitched a little, as if his somewhat pointed question had hit home. "No, not really," she admitted after a moment. "A hike could be fun."

He hoped his smile didn't look smug, but he was pleased that she had accepted his invitation. "I'll see you in the morning, then. I'll pick you up at nine o'clock?"

She nodded. "I'll be ready."

He brushed her cheek with his hand again, not to tuck back her hair this time, but simply to enjoy the feel of her soft skin. "Let your problems go for a while," he said lightly. "Have some fun. You'll know what to do when it's time."

Her eyes narrowed and she pulled back. "What do you mean? You haven't been talking about me behind my back, have you?"

Giving an exaggerated sigh, he shook his head. "I know nothing about you that you haven't told me yourself, or that I haven't observed while I've been with you. I can just tell that something is causing you stress. I hope you can leave it behind tomorrow and have a little fun."

She looked at him a moment longer, then gave a rather weary-looking smile and said, "Thanks. I'll try."

He caught just a hint of the dimples at the corners of her mouth. Just enough to make him want to see them again.

He cleared his throat and forced himself to move away from

her before he forgot that he was trying to be a gentleman. "Okay then, see you in the morning."

"Good night, Casey."

"Good night." Hearing the door close behind him, he moved thoughtfully toward his truck. So maybe the evening had almost ended awkwardly, thanks to his poorly timed advice to her. But he would be seeing Natalie again in the morning.

That prospect made him feel just a little too eager for his own peace of mind.

Natalie yanked on the laces of her left hiking boot with a bit more force than necessary, tying them tightly enough to cut off the circulation in her foot. And then she loosened them a little because her self-recriminations didn't extend to inflicting actual pain.

It wasn't that she was annoyed with herself for agreeing to go hiking with Casey. Though it had been a while since she'd been, she liked to hike. And she was the first to admit that she needed to get out of the cabin, spend a day doing something else, getting some fresh air, trying to clear her mind. Casey would be an entertaining companion, the pleasant diversion she had acknowledged needing and which he didn't seem to mind providing.

What really irked her about last night was that she had been so out of control of her emotions that she'd allowed Casey to see that she was wrestling with a problem. She'd let herself drink too much, something she almost never did, and apparently her unguarded expressions had given away much more than she had intended. She must have looked pathetic. Casey hadn't asked her any personal questions, but he'd made it clear that he'd noticed her behavior and that he was sympathetic, if not outright curious.

She wondered why he hadn't kissed her when he left, when they both knew he had wanted to.

Shaking her head impatiently, she put thoughts of kissing Casey out of her mind. For now.

She could only hope he wouldn't start asking questions today. She wouldn't lie to him, but she didn't want to talk about what had happened, either. Even though she suspected that he would be a very good listener. And she couldn't help being curious about him and what he was running from back in Dallas.

For their outing, she wore a long-sleeve white pullover with a high-necked, half-zip front, slim navy hiking pants, a quilted red vest and mid-height hiking boots. Her hair was too short for a ponytail, but she'd topped it with a red baseball cap to keep it out of her face. The weather was predicted to be cool, in the low 60s. It would be even cooler in the higher elevations, so she had tried to dress appropriately.

Ready a little early, she decided to try to call Beecham again. Because of the one-hour time difference, it was quite early in Nashville, but she didn't care if she woke him. She needed to know that he, at least, was making some progress while she whiled away the morning with Casey.

Expecting his voice mail again, she was pleased when he answered, instead. "Rand Beecham," he said briskly, as if he'd been up for hours.

Because she had no doubt that he'd checked his caller ID before answering, she wasn't particularly impressed. "It's Natalie Lofton," she said, anyway. "I haven't heard from you in several days. What have you found out?"

"I'm following several leads, Ms. Lofton. Several very promising leads."

"Like what?"

"Like there's a woman in your firm who's suddenly come into some money."

"I'm aware of that. Everyone knows that. Have you found out where the money came from?"

"I can't prove anything yet, but don't you worry. I'll find out what's going on. Just give me another few days to put together a strong case."

Another few days to bill her account, she added silently with a frown, not to mention the fairly sizable amount she'd paid up-front. She wished she had more experience with this sort of thing, but she tended to focus more on the business aspect of the law. Contracts, prenups, bankruptcies… hired snoops were hardly her area of expertise. "Mr. Beecham, I must insist that you provide some results soon or I'll have to find someone else who can. My career is on hold until you find who framed me. I can't afford to wait much longer, for several reasons."

"I'm on that, Ms. Lofton. I'll call you as soon as I've got what you're looking for, okay?"

She would have liked to push him more, but a tapping on her door let her know that Casey had arrived. Telling Beecham she expected to hear from him soon, she disconnected, completely dissatisfied with the conversation.

Trying to smooth the frown from her face, she moved to open the door.

Casey wore jeans, a denim jacket over a gray pullover and sneakers. "Whoa," he said when she opened the door to him. "You look great. Very hiker chic."

He could make her smile, even when she was still stinging from the way she'd behaved the night before, and still brooding over her less-than-satisfactory conversation with Beecham. "Thank you. Actually, I haven't been hiking in years. I bought this outfit last year when I was planning a vacation that fell through. It's nice to have a chance to wear it."

"How long has it been since you've been on a vacation?"

She wrinkled her nose. "Longer than I like to admit."

Chuckling, he made a motion toward his truck. "Then let's go have some fun."

She snatched up the small nylon backpack she'd prepared for the hike. "I brought a very light lunch in case we get hungry," she told him, slinging the bag over her shoulder.

He grinned as they fell in step toward his truck. "We won't go hungry. I've got a pack with some granola bars and bottles of water. I wasn't sure what else to bring."

He opened the passenger door of his truck for her, and she climbed in, reaching for the seat belt when he closed the door. He loped around the front of the truck, slid behind the wheel and fastened himself in before starting the engine. "Do you have a favorite trail?"

"I looked up a few online last night. Tommy's favorite was the Ramsey Cascades Trail. He took me on that one a couple of times when I was a kid, and the cascades at the end of the graded trail are spectacular. The hiking guides list it as 'moderate to strenuous' in difficulty. It's pretty steep, rising more than two thousand feet in four miles. The guidebook said it's an eight mile round-trip, about a five-hour hike on average. Or there's an easier trail…"

"That one sounds nice," he said, putting the truck in Reverse. "I've got a few extra hours today. I'd like to see the cascades."

She nodded. The memories of that trail were bittersweet, but she would like to see the falls again. She remembered thinking they had to be the most beautiful place on earth. She could use some natural beauty today.

"Which way do I turn?" Casey asked, pausing at the end of the driveway.

"Left," she said, and sat back in her seat.

He was right, she decided. She needed to forget about her problems and have fun today. She deserved that, darn it.

Looking at his attractive profile from beneath her lashes, she decided she had chosen exactly the right companion for a day of determinedly carefree fun.

Casey couldn't decide which was more beautiful—the stunning mountain scenery on the trail, or Natalie. He finally decided it was almost a tie, with her having just a slight edge, at least as far as he was concerned.

The trail began as an old gravel logging road through the forest running alongside a tumbling stream that Natalie called "The Ramsey Prong" of the Little Pigeon River. In the summer, Casey imagined the trail would be shady and very green. As it was, there was still some color in the leaves that rained down on them with every cool breeze.

The gravel road was surrounded by mossy fallen tree trunks and enormous boulders, but not particularly steep yet. She had warned him that it got much steeper when the old road ended and the trail became a worn footpath.

"In the summer there are wildflowers through here," she said, gesturing toward the leaf-strewn forest floor, her thin digital camera in her other hand. "Little violets and irises and other things I never learned to identify."

"There are probably more hikers in the summer, too," he commented, and though he spoke quietly, his voice sounded almost loud in the hushed forest. It felt as if he and Natalie were the only ones on the mountain, but he'd seen a couple other cars in the lot when they'd parked.

"Oh, yes, especially during the weekends. This is nice, isn't it? Having the trail pretty much to ourselves?"

He put a hand lightly at the small of her back, ostensibly to help her around a boulder, mostly just because he wanted to touch her. "Yeah. It's very nice."

It pleased him that she made no effort to move away from his hand as they continued to walk, stepping ahead only when the path grew too narrow to navigate side by side.

He lifted an eyebrow when they came to a footbridge over the stream. The bridge was a long, somewhat bouncy-looking, narrow log with a single handrail. Water tumbled noisily over boulders beneath the bridge—and the water looked cold.

Lowering her camera after taking a shot of the bridge, Natalie looked back at him. "Problem?"

"No. Just hoping the traction on these shoes is all the ads claim it to be."

She laughed. "Come on. I promise not to push you in. As long as you behave."

Was that a hint for him to keep his hands to himself? Watching her delicately crossing the bridge, he told himself it might be worth a cold dunking to touch her again.

"Smile," she said from the other side of the prong.

Posing in the middle of the bridge, he grinned as she snapped his picture.

"Man, these trees are huge," he commented a few minutes later as the trail wound between massive trunks. Gnarled roots snaked across the worn path, waiting to snag a carelessly placed foot or twist an ankle. Patches of moss added to the challenge, which was why, he supposed, the guidebooks rated this hike as strenuous. That, and the increase in altitude.

Natalie placed her hand on the rough bark of a tree that had to be twelve feet in diameter. "Yellow poplars. This is virgin forest. Beautiful, isn't it?"

Frowning at some initials clumsily carved into the bark of another massive tree, he nodded. "Wonder why some people can't appreciate nature's beauty without making their own marks on it."

"Or leaving their trash behind," she agreed with a look of distaste. "Nothing makes me madder than to see a beautiful place soiled with beer bottles and aluminum cans."

They pulled water bottles out of their packs and took a few sips while they looked around. "How far do you think we've walked?" he asked, guessing at a couple of miles.

"About two and a half miles, I think," she hazarded, confirming his own guess. "A little over halfway."

Capping her water bottle, she returned it to her pack, then raised the camera and focused on a tangle of roots with wild fern growing among them. He'd noticed that she had a flair for photography; she'd taken some interesting shots during their walk so far. He would have to ask for copies.

"Natalie." He nudged her arm and pointed to where two wild turkeys strutted across the path.

She swung the camera in that direction, snapping a couple of shots before the big birds fluttered into the woods. "Cool," she said, lowering the camera with a smile.

He took the camera from her hand and stepped back. "Stand in front of those two black cherry trees," he instructed. "Right between them. Yes, there."

He took the picture, then glanced at the screen on the back of the camera. "Nice. Now move over there, by the water."

She shook her head, but obliged, anyway. "I didn't bring the camera so I'd have a lot of pictures of me."

"I don't know why not. You've been taking shots of natural beauty all day."

She groaned and snatched the camera away from him, leaving him grinning as they started walking again. He was almost sure she'd had to struggle not to smile in response to his corny quip.

They crossed another log bridge and walked between two

more large poplars, where they encountered a doe quietly foraging for vegetation. She looked up at them, waited politely for Natalie to snap her picture, then bounded away in graceful leaps, leaving her human admirers smiling. A squirrel barked in a tree above them, and Casey looked up to see it watching them and twitching its tail. "The wildlife out here is certainly accustomed to people."

"Considering how many thousands take this hike every year, it's no wonder," Natalie replied. She zipped the front of her bright red vest. "It's getting cooler as we climb higher, isn't it?"

"Are you cold? You can wear my jacket."

"Thanks, but I'm fine. This vest is actually pretty warm. We've only got about a mile to go before we reach the falls."

He stepped carefully over a pile of somewhat slippery rocks. "I'm really glad we decided to do this. It feels good to get away from everything for a while."

She took the hand he extended to help her over the rocks. "It does feel good," she acknowledged, and then smiled ruefully. "I have to admit I'm a little out of shape. Too much desk time, not enough gym time the past couple of years."

It might have been a good time to slip in a question about what she'd done at that desk, but Casey decided to let the moment pass. All he wanted to do now was to enjoy this day. This moment. And he suspected Natalie felt the same way.

"Your shape looks good to me," he said, earning himself another groan—and another fleeting glimpse of dimples.

She glanced down. "You're still holding my hand," she pointed out.

He tightened his fingers just a little. "I know. It's a very nice hand."

Lacing her fingers with his, she smiled. "You're flirting."

"So, you noticed this time."

She looked up at him through her lashes, which made his pulse rate flutter a little in response. A typical male response to a very feminine look, he thought, even as she murmured, "I've noticed before."

His face was close to hers now, their lips only a few inches apart. "And did you like it?"

With a laugh, she disentangled their hands and took a step away, lifting her camera to snap his picture. "Let's keep moving," she said, turning to head up the trail again.

Grinning in intrigue, he followed her.

The trail narrowed again and rose even more steeply as they neared the end. They'd been accompanied almost all the way by the sounds of water—rushing, tumbling, spilling over small ledges, gurgling in pools—but now Casey could hear a distinctive waterfall roar, as he thought of it. They climbed over a few more fallen trees, hopped across a couple more rocks, and then they were at their destination. And it was everything Natalie had promised it would be.

"Wow," he said, raising his voice a little to be heard over the noise. "This is amazing."

Breathing a little hard from the challenge of the last part of the trail, she smiled. "I told you."

The cascades, formed by the joining of two separate creeks at the top, tumbled ninety feet downward over a series of rock ledges into a clear pool at the bottom. Signs were posted around the area warning hikers not to try to climb the ledges, as several people had died trying to do so. Feeling the cold, breeze-borne spray on his face, Casey wasn't even tempted to do anything so foolish. Just seeing this place was reward enough for the strenuous hike.

He turned to Natalie, who'd found a flat-topped boulder on which to rest. Her cheeks were red and she was still breathing a bit more quickly than usual, but she seemed to be rapidly recovering. She gazed at the falls with an expression that made him think she was seeing it both in the present and in her memories of earlier hikes with the late cousin she had obviously loved.

Sensing that he was looking at her, she met his eyes with a slight smile. "It didn't take me as long to catch my breath when I came up here as a kid," she admitted, wrinkling her nose in a way that he found very appealing. "And don't think I haven't noticed that you aren't even breathing hard."

He shrugged. "I've been doing a lot of manual labor lately."

"Not to mention that you're almost four years younger than I am," she grumbled.

Laughing, he settled beside her on the boulder. "Like that's enough to matter."

She made a sound he couldn't quite interpret, and then she swung her little backpack around in front of her and pulled out her water bottle again. "Are you hungry?"

"I could eat."

She dug in the pack and started pulling out the food she'd brought along. They spent the next half hour eating in the damp, chilly air beside the cascades, enjoying the scenery and the companionship. Casey doubted that they'd have been lucky enough to have the site to themselves had it been a weekend, or a summer day. Which made him even more glad that he and Natalie had chosen a November Monday morning for their excursion. He liked being alone with her here.

They stuffed their trash into a plastic bag Natalie had brought for that purpose, then put that back into her backpack, making sure they left no trace of their visit behind. Fully rested now, Natalie took some pictures of the cascades and of Casey posed in front of them, and then he returned the favor, snapping several shots of her.

"That's enough," she said when he'd taken the third picture of her. "We'd probably better head back now."

She started to move toward him, but her left foot slipped on a wet, mossy rock. She stumbled forward, then fell, landing solidly on her right hip.

Casey had tried to catch her, but he just hadn't been fast enough. He reached her almost the moment she made contact with the ground. "Natalie? Are you okay?"

Looking thoroughly embarrassed, she nodded, reaching for her cap, which had fallen off in her tumble. "I'm fine. Just lost my footing. Stupid."

"It could have been worse," he said, his pulse rate still a bit too fast. "You could have fallen backward."

She glanced at the falls behind them and made a face. "That would definitely have been worse."

"Can you stand?"

"Of course. I'm fine, Casey, really."

"Here, let me help you." Setting the camera aside, he took her left arm and supported her while she rose unsteadily to her feet. The way she winced when she put weight on her right leg told him that she was hurt a bit worse than she wanted him to know, but a few tentative steps convinced him that nothing was broken or even sprained.

He kept his hand on her arm until she was on more even ground. She glanced up at him with an awkward smile. "I really am okay," she assured him again. "I'm going to have a very colorful bruise, but that's the extent of it."

"Probably going to be sore, too."

She shrugged. "That was already inevitable after the hike."

She'd put her cap back on a bit crookedly. He reached up to straighten it, tucking her honey-blond hair away from her face. The gesture brought him closer to her and she tipped her head back to look at him from beneath the brim of her red cap. She stood very still as he traced a fingertip down her jawline, wiping a smudge of dirt from her chin.

"Bet you thought I'd be the one to wipe out today," he teased quietly, hoping to make her smile again.

She did. "I guess we're both a little accident-prone."

He chuckled. "Maybe."

"Of course, the hike isn't over yet. You could still 'wipe out.'"

"I do have a tendency to press my luck," he admitted, his hand still touching her face. He spread his fingers until his palm cupped her cheek. "Gets me in trouble sometimes."

She made a slight sound that might have been a swallowed laugh. "I can see that."

"Sometimes it's worth it," he murmured, lowering his head. Holding her gaze with his own, he said, "You never answered my question earlier."

"Which question?" she asked, tilting her head back a little more.

"Do you like it when I flirt with you? Because, you know, I'll stop if you don't."

She gave a little shrug. "There's no need to stop. I like it well enough."

Amused by her nonchalant tone, he said, "Let me guess. I'm a pleasant diversion."

"You could put it that way."

Grinning, he spoke against her lips. "I've got no complaints about that."

Chapter Six

Rationally, Natalie knew this was risky. The timing was terrible, and she wasn't the vacation-fling type, anyway. But the truth was, kissing Casey felt too darned good. As she had suspected it would.

He lifted his head slowly, his gaze locked with hers. "Going to push me into the water now?"

She slid her hand around the back of his neck. "Maybe later," she said and pulled his mouth to hers again.

He smiled for a moment against her lips, until the kiss deepened and amusement faded into something very different. Natalie felt her breathing start to quicken again, but this time she couldn't blame it on exertion or altitude. This reaction was due totally to Casey.

The sound of voices mingled with the rush of water, seeping into her consciousness. Someone laughed, and she and Casey broke apart, staggering backward as if caught doing something they shouldn't. Rubbing her sore thigh, she looked toward the trail just in time to see two couples in their late teens or early twenties climb into sight. They were chattering and laughing and roughhousing a little, and seemed to be having a great time. And not one of the fit-looking foursome appeared to be at all winded by the climb, Natalie noted with a frown.

The newcomers greeted Natalie and Casey with friendly nods, then moved to the side of the cascades to exclaim excitedly over the view. Natalie and Casey shared a glance, then moved in unspoken unison toward the trail.

The return drive to the cabin was quiet, but not uncomfortably so. Natalie sat back in her seat, watching the passing mountainsides, occasionally looking at Casey. He caught her gaze at times and smiled. They talked about how much fun they'd had, the beautiful trail, what a joy it had been to reach the falls. They didn't specifically mention the kisses they had shared, but she had no doubt that he was thinking about them, just as she was.

Casey parked in front of her cabin and turned off the truck. "I'll put the furniture back on the deck before I leave."

"I'll help you."

"Thanks. I could use your help with the table, especially."

They went inside only long enough to freshen up and for Natalie to make a pot of coffee. They drank half a cup each, just for the energy boost, and then she poured the rest into an insulated carafe for drinking later. Casey went out to get started on the deck, and she followed him after changing from her hiking boots into more comfortable sneakers.

They had just replaced the last chair when Casey looked past her and smiled. "The dog's back. Want to bring some fresh water and a bowl for the food I brought?"

She'd almost forgotten about the dog. "I'll be right back."

The dog waited by the edge of the woods, watching them with the now-familiar wary anticipation. Casey set the bowls on the ground, talking in the quietly reassuring voice he used with the stray. "It's dry food today, not fancy meat, but it's better for you. More of the nutrients you need. So try it before you turn up your nose, okay?"

Natalie smiled. The dog wasn't in a position to turn up its nose at any kind of food. It attacked the dry food as hungrily as it had the meat loaf and pot roast, crunching noisily as it gulped down the meal.

"He is a boy," Casey murmured, having caught a glimpse of something Natalie couldn't see because of all the matted fur.

"So you guessed correctly."

"He just acted like another guy. Right, buddy?"

Still chewing, the dog glanced at Casey and gave a quick wave of its tail.

Natalie and Casey looked at each other in surprise. "Did you see that?" he asked.

"I did. He wagged his tail. I think he's starting to respond to you."

"Maybe he is, a little." Taking a step closer to the dog, Casey crouched and held out a hand.

The dog glanced at that hand, then at Casey's face. He stretched out his head a couple of inches and sniffed the air around Casey's hand. His tail wagged a couple more times. Natalie held her breath. She didn't think the dog was in any way aggressive, but she still felt as if Casey was taking a risk reaching out that way.

The dog looked up at Casey from beneath what, to Natalie, looked like beetled brows. As if it were trying to gauge Casey's motivations. And then it took a step closer to him.

Very carefully, moving very slowly, Casey touched the dog's

head. He spoke in a low voice, "That's a good boy. We're getting to be friends, aren't we? You just need to learn to trust me a little."

The dog wagged its tail once more, before moving back. He eyed Casey for another minute, glanced at Natalie, then turned and trotted away. Natalie couldn't imagine why the past few moments had left her with a lump in her throat.

Straightening, Casey smiled at her, and she thought she saw a hint of her own emotions in his eyes. "He's getting there," he said.

"Yes, I suppose he is. How long do you think it will take until he's ready to be placed in a home? Or at least a shelter for the winter?"

"I'll give it another couple of days, while I finish up the work here. In the meantime, I'll ask Kyle if he knows anyone who might be interested in taking the dog in."

"It's starting to get dark. I have some food ready to heat. I thought you might be hungry early since we had such a light lunch."

"As a matter of fact, I'm starving," he admitted. "I could almost eat a bowl of that kibble."

She laughed. "You won't have to resort to that. I'll heat one of Aunt Jewel's famous chicken casseroles."

"Sounds great." He turned with her toward the house, each of them carrying one of the bowls in which they'd served the stray food and water. "I've got to wash my hands. Our dog needs a bath."

Something about the way he said "our dog" took her aback. That sounded just a bit too cozy for her comfort, though she doubted that he'd meant it quite that way.

They talked about Casey's work schedule during dinner. He would be over early the next morning, he said, to begin caulking, a job that would take at least a full day. Window washing and the hot tub installation were also on his To-Do list for the week.

"That sounds like a lot," Natalie commented, trying not to sound envious that he had worthwhile things to do.

He shrugged. "I like to stay busy."

"So do I," she murmured, looking away from him.

He waited a beat, then asked casually, "How's the job search going?"

She couldn't meet his eyes as she replied, "I'm waiting to hear from some people."

"I see. Well, I hope you find what you're looking for soon."

"Yes, so do I. Would you like some more coffee?"

He shook his head. "No, I've had plenty. I guess I'll head home."

Home. Though she knew it was just a figure of speech, she found it rather odd that he referred to his temporary cabin that way. Didn't he miss his life in Dallas? His family and friends? He certainly didn't talk about his life there much, not that she had exactly encouraged discussions about their lives before they'd met.

She stood, then winced when her bruised thigh protested the movement. She should have known Casey wouldn't miss that telltale expression.

"Are you hurting?"

She shook her head. "Just a little sore from my fall. It's nothing, only a bruise."

"Bet you wish that hot tub was already installed, don't you?" he teased.

She smiled. "It would probably feel good tonight. But I suppose I'll make do with a hot bath, instead."

He had followed her to the sink, carrying his plate and utensils from dinner. When she turned, he was right there, standing so close they were almost touching, his gaze locked with hers in a way that made her breath catch.

"Am I going to get my face slapped if I say I wouldn't mind joining you in a hot tub sometime?" he asked, his tone somehow whimsical and serious all at the same time.

"I don't slap," she replied a bit huskily. "I punch."

He laughed. "Of course you do."

And then his smile faded as he reached up to touch a corner of her mouth. "Have I mentioned how much I like these dimples?"

"You're flirting again."

He grinned. "I do have permission."

She rested her hands on his chest. "So you do."

He kissed her lingeringly. Her fingers clenched in his shirt. The man definitely knew how to kiss. Flexing her fingers, she noted the strength of the muscles beneath his shirt. Maybe he didn't do a lot of manual labor, but he certainly stayed in fine shape. If a woman happened to be in the market for a vacation fling with a good-looking, great-kissing, charmingly entertaining young stud, Casey Walker was darn near the perfect choice.

Lifting his head very slowly, he smiled down at her, his eyes gleaming in a way that made her wonder if he was more talented at mind reading than maintenance work.

"I'm sure you're tired," he said. "I should probably go."

Though feminine instinct urged her to detain him longer, she moistened her well-kissed lips and nodded with some reluctance. "That's probably a good idea."

She walked with him to the door. "Good night, Natalie," he said from the open doorway. "I really enjoyed the hike. Thanks for letting me go along. Oh, and thanks again for dinner."

"You're welcome. For both."

He looked at her mouth, then back up at her eyes. And then he gave a firm little nod, and closed the door behind him, refusing to give in to the temptation that she hoped had been as strong for him as it was for her.

Hearing his truck engine fade away down the mountainside, Natalie lifted a hand to her mouth. Oddly enough, she felt as though he had kissed her good-night with just a look.

Casey Walker was definitely proving to be a distraction. Much more than she had planned on, she was afraid.

Because it was still relatively early, Casey stopped by to talk to Kyle after leaving Natalie. He'd called first to make sure it was a good time, and Kyle had assured him that it was. Molly opened the door to him, greeting him with a smile and a kiss on the cheek. "Come in. Kyle's reading Olivia her bedtime story. He'll be down when he's finished. How was your hike today?"

"We had a great time," Casey replied, taking a seat in the living room with his cousin. "Beautiful scenery. Have you been up to the cascades?"

"Yes, Kyle and I went there once. It was breathtaking."

"Really is. Well worth the trek up."

"Did Natalie have a good time?"

"She seemed to."

"Good. She needs to have little fun. She just seems so sad."

Sad. It was a good word for what Casey, himself, had sensed in Natalie from the start. "I think she enjoyed the outing," he said again, not knowing what else to say, since he had assured Natalie he wasn't asking questions behind her back.

"Good. And maybe she'll find a new job soon. I don't know what happened, exactly, but Jewel was always talking about what a great position her niece had with that fancy law firm in Nashville. It must have been a bitter split for Natalie to be taking it so hard."

As much as he had told himself he wouldn't ask any questions, Casey couldn't stop himself from asking, "Wait—Natalie worked for a law firm?"

"She's a lawyer—like you. I, um, thought you knew that."

"No," he said grimly. "No, I didn't."

"Oh." Molly bit her lip. "Maybe she didn't want to talk about it. Maybe since you've still got that great position with the firm in Dallas—"

"We haven't talked about jobs. She might not know what I do. Unless you've told her?"

"No, it never came up."

"Well then, unless her aunt has mentioned it—"

"Jewel doesn't know what you do for a living. You said you didn't want to talk about work while you were here, so I just didn't mention it."

"So I guess Natalie doesn't know."

"No, probably not."

"So, maybe we should just keep it that way for now."

Molly lifted her eyebrows. "You don't want to tell her?"

"I don't want anyone else to tell her," he corrected. "I mean, if she's lost her position and is still upset about it, she's probably not going to want to hear that the maintenance guy is an attorney with a big firm in Dallas."

"Oh. Well, I guess that makes sense. I'll tell Kyle to be sure and let you be the one to bring it up with her."

"Thanks."

"Speaking of your job, and I don't mean the maintenance work…"

"Don't you start, too," Casey warned with a frown.

She blinked her big green eyes at him in a patented innocent-Molly look. "Start what?"

"Nagging me about going back to work. Mom calls every

morning, Dad calls at night. Jason, Aaron and Andrew take the tag-team approach, and most of the aunts have checked in at least once while I've been here. Everyone's afraid I've had a meltdown or something, and they all want to pipe in with advice before I ruin my life. The only ones who don't seem concerned that I've taken a long vacation are my superiors at the firm."

"Your superiors are hoping the vacation will help get your head together so you can come back in top form again. They know they have a potential gold mine in you, and they don't want to give up on it too quickly."

He shrugged, but he had to acknowledge she was probably right, as she so often was. Like her mother, Molly had a talent for cutting through the b.s. and getting straight to the heart of a discussion.

"You can't really blame the family, though," she continued. "It was unexpected of you to just drop everything and take off the way you did. They can't help worrying that the setbacks you've had during the past few months have shaken your confidence in yourself. You know how strongly the Walkers believe in getting right back on the horse that threw you."

How many times had he heard that adage growing up? He shook his head in bemusement. "So what do *you* think?"

"I don't think you've lost your confidence," she replied after a moment. "Losing that big case—well, that's part of the job, and you know that. No matter how well you prepare, how passionately you believe in your client, how hard you work to get the win, sometimes you're just going to lose. I think you were bummed about it, especially since it was such a high-profile case, but I don't believe it destroyed your confidence or anything like that.

"As for the breakup with Tamara," she continued matter-of-factly, "I don't think that was particularly devastating to you, either. Truth is, I've thought for a while that you were with her more out of habit and everyone else's expectations than because you were really in love with her. When you told me she'd broken it off with you, you sounded more relieved than upset, though you're too nice a guy to admit, even to yourself, that you were glad it was over after such a long time together."

He shifted uncomfortably on the couch. Maybe Molly was a bit too perceptive. He'd only admitted to himself recently that the breakup with Tamara had been a relief, in a way. He'd tried so hard during the past year to keep her happy and keep their relationship together that he hadn't spent enough time asking himself if that was what he really wanted. But it still stung that after all he'd done, she hadn't even had the decency to leave him before she'd started seeing someone else behind his back.

Molly wasn't quite finished. "I think everyone else is so busy focusing on those big things, naturally enough, that they missed the real incident that left you questioning yourself and the path you've been on."

He studied her with narrowed eyes. "What do you mean?" he asked, though he was afraid he already knew.

Her face soft with sympathy, Molly laid a hand on his knee. "It wasn't your fault, Casey. You didn't put Ian Duvall in that car that night."

His throat tightened, making him speak in a growl. "I might as well have."

Her fingers tightened. "No. You did your job. You got him acquitted on those earlier charges."

Casey swallowed. "I knew he was guilty."

"You did your job," she repeated firmly. "It wasn't your place to decide guilt or innocence. It was the jury's. And they decided to acquit him."

"Because I did my job so damned well."

"Exactly. The fact that he chose—he *chose*, Casey—to drive drunk less than a year later had nothing to do with you."

Giving his knee one last pat, she sat back. "You needed this vacation. Needed a chance to think, away from the craziness back home. I don't think that's so strange. And heaven knows we needed your help right now. So don't let everyone else make you question yourself, okay? Do what you have to do."

Molly knew all about following her own path. To the consternation of almost the entire Walker clan, she'd left her family ranch, the teaching position she'd held there and everything she'd known back in Dallas to move to Gatlinburg with Kyle. Though she would always be close to her family, Casey didn't think she'd had one day of regret about leaving behind the life she'd always expected to have among them in Texas.

Maybe that was part of what had drawn him to Molly when he'd made his great escape. She had made a huge change that had left everyone else bewildered and worried, and it had worked out for her. He wasn't saying that he wanted to make a huge change, really—he wasn't sure yet just what he wanted—but it was nice to see that it could be done, and successfully, by someone from the same family boat in which he'd been floating so safely for the past twenty-six years.

Do what you have to do. Sounded simple enough. Now all he had to do was figure out what that was.

Natalie was on the phone with Amber when she heard Casey's truck in the drive the next morning. Her pulse rate jumped involuntarily, but she made an effort to concentrate on the call.

"So Cathy's sporting some new clothes," she said as a way of reminding herself what they'd been talking about.

"A whole new wardrobe," Amber emphasized. "Not just a

few new sweaters or anything. And from what I can tell, she's scored some expensive designer stuff."

"And she hasn't said where all this money is coming from?"

"No. She just giggles whenever anyone asks and sort of coyly says she's found a new source of income. She won't say anything more about it. Which makes me wonder if her new source of income is selling client information to the tabloids."

"What bothers me is that she's so open about the spending," Natalie fretted. "Is she really foolish enough to brag in the firm if she's making the money by exploiting her job?"

"Have you met Cathy?" Amber asked drily. "She's stupid enough to think no one would even notice."

"Has anyone noticed? Anyone in the upper tiers of the firm, I mean, not the other clerical staff."

"I don't know. If they have, nothing's been done. I mean, she's still here."

Natalie sighed in frustration. "And I suppose there have been no more information leaks since I left."

"None," Amber said, sounding almost apologetic. "The leaks stopped the day you left."

"Which only makes me look more guilty."

"I, um…"

"Never mind." There really was nothing Amber could say to make this situation any better. "I know you need to get to work. Thanks for calling."

"I just wanted to check on you. You're sure you're okay?"

"I'm fine." She was already hearing noises from outside that indicated Casey had started working. "Really."

"I hope you took my advice the last time we talked. Have you done something fun while you're there?"

"I went hiking yesterday, actually. I had a very nice time."

"Hey, that's great. Got any big plans for today?"

Another thump sounded from outside. "There are a few things I could do," she replied vaguely.

"Good. Take advantage of the time off. I'd love to be in a cabin in the Smokies right now instead of just about to start a day of boring filing."

"Yes, well…"

"Have you heard from any other firms yet? I mean, you are sending out résumés, aren't you?"

"I haven't heard anything yet," Natalie said evasively. She saw no need to mention that she hadn't quite gotten up the nerve to send out any inquiries yet. How could she, before she'd found some way of clearing her name? Who would hire her now?

"Well, hang in there, okay? You'll find something. You're too good at what you do not to. Not everyone's going to believe the accusations against you, especially after they meet you and realize you're not like that."

Natalie wasn't so sure of that.

They disconnected only moments later. Natalie tried immediately to call Beecham, but was routed to his voice mail again, to her annoyance. Tossing the cell phone aside, she rubbed her temples where a dull ache threatened. A tapping sound made her look up, and her eyes met Casey's through the sliding glass door that led out to the deck. Seeing his look of concern, she pasted on a smile and moved to open the door.

Chapter Seven

"Are you okay?" Casey asked before she could even speak.

"Yes, I'm fine. A little headache."

He didn't seem entirely reassured, and she wondered just how disheartened she'd appeared after her talk with Amber. "Is there something you need?" she asked to change the subject.

"Yeah. The dog bowls."

"He's back?"

"Yes."

"He's earlier than usual."

"He's hungry, I guess."

She moved toward the kitchen. "I'll get the bowls."

The dog sat at the edge of the woods again, but maybe a bit closer to the cabin than he'd ventured before. His tail wagged against the ground when Casey and Natalie brought the bowls. And Natalie would have sworn the dog smiled just a little when they set them in front of him.

The dog ate part of the food, and drank a little of the water. And then he just sat there, watching them.

"He doesn't seem to be as hungry as he has been," Natalie remarked.

"Well, yeah. We've been feeding him. Maybe he just wanted to make sure we were still here with the food."

"Maybe he did." She studied the dog, then on impulse knelt down and held out her hand.

"Hi, buddy," she said, using the same soft tone and nickname that Casey always employed with the stray. "Have you figured out we're not going to hurt you?"

It was almost as if he'd been waiting for her to reach out. The dog rose, walked straight toward her, sniffed her fingers, then licked her hand. His tail wagged behind him as he gazed up at her with what could only be called a melting look.

"Wow," Casey said, sounding both startled and amused. "He's certainly taking to you. Are you wearing beef-scented perfume or something today?"

Tentatively, she patted the dog's dirty head. The matted tail wagged more eagerly. "I don't think he understands that I'm not really a dog person."

"He thinks you are." Casey knelt beside her and the dog sniffed his hand, then allowed Casey to pet him briefly on the head. And then the dog turned back to Natalie, moving closer to her, his body touching her knees.

Though the mutt was in dire need of a bath, Natalie didn't recoil. A little dirt wouldn't hurt her jeans. And she had to admit that she was rather touched that he seemed to have taken to her. Maybe it would be easier to find a good home for him if they could convince him that humans could be nice to have around. "How old do you think he is?"

"A year, maybe? Year-and-a-half at the most."

"I wonder if he's ever had a home."

"My guess would be yes. I think he's been socialized at some point. He was probably dumped or abandoned when someone moved or when he got bigger than expected or maybe they just got tired of him. Or maybe he got lost and never found his way back home again."

"Do you think someone is looking for him?"

"No collar. And he's ragged enough that he looks like he's been on his own for a while. So, no, probably not."

Giving the mutt one last pat, she rose from the uncomfortable crouch. The dog gazed up at her, then trotted over to take another drink, after which he curled in the sun and watched them from sleepy-lidded eyes.

"Doesn't look like he's going anywhere for now," Casey commented. "He's staying near the food."

"Have you mentioned him to Kyle or Molly yet? To see if they know someone who would be willing to take him?"

"No, not yet. I wanted to see if he showed the potential to be a family pet. After this morning, I'm thinking yes."

She looked back over her shoulder as they moved toward the house. The dog lay in his sunny spot, his eyes closed now. The air was chilly, and the ground was probably still cold from the night, but he seemed to be getting enough warmth from the bright morning sun to keep him comfortable. "He'd probably be more appealing to a potential owner if he had a bath."

"We'll take it one step at a time for now."

That sounded like a good idea—in a lot of ways, she decided.

She looked at the ladder and caulking supplies sitting by the side of the cabin where Casey had been working before he'd spotted the dog. "Is there anything I can do to help?"

"Sure, if you're looking for something to do."

She nodded on a sudden decision. "I'd like to help."

Anything to get her out of that house. Away from the computer that was doing her so little good. Away from the phone that remained frustratingly silent, except from the occasional call from Amber. And distracted from the nagging fears that she was going to run out of savings before she cleared her name and found another position.

"You might want to get a jacket. And your gloves. Maybe a cap."

"Can I bring you anything?"

"I'm okay for now."

"Then I'll be right back."

She was inside less than ten minutes. Returning with her gloves, she came to a stop on the deck when she saw that the dog had moved closer to the cabin and was now sitting only a few yards from the steps, gazing expectantly up at her. "I didn't bring you any more food, Buddy."

"He's been sitting there ever since you went inside. I just looked around and there he was. What did you do, hypnotize him?"

"I didn't do anything. You were the one who talked to him most and fed him and everything."

Shrugging, Casey quipped, "Guess he just fell under your irresistible spell."

She rolled her eyes. "Let's get to work, shall we?"

Casey laughed and turned with her toward the cabin. The dog curled up nearby, apparently content to be near them and the food without being too close for his own comfort level.

Had anyone asked, Natalie would have had a hard time explaining how she and Casey ended up visiting the large aquarium in downtown Gatlinburg at six that evening. They'd finished working on the cabin only an hour earlier, and here they were, walking into a popular tourist attraction.

She wasn't even sure who'd first mentioned the aquarium, though she knew Casey was the one who'd suggested they visit after she admitted that she loved them. He hadn't even had to work very hard to convince her to agree. She had looked at the empty cabin waiting for her and then at Casey's smiling face, and she'd weighed her choices. Obsessing about her problems— or spending a few hours in an aquarium with a very likable and attractive man. It was a no-brainer, really.

She spent the next two hours laughing. A lot. She laughed at the "fishy-faces" Casey made at the colorful inhabitants of the many tanks. She laughed when he held a horseshoe crab and talked her into holding one, too. She laughed when he reached down to pat a ray in a sandy-bottomed petting tank and got splashed in the face when one of the rays playfully slapped the water with a broad wing.

They stared mesmerized at the otherworldly jellyfish undulating through water to the strains of piped-in, new age music. They rode the moving walkway through a long Plexiglas tube that gave them up-close views of sharks swimming toward them and over their heads. They oohed and aahed over the vivid colors and spectacular markings of the many different types of fish in the tropical displays. They admired sea horses and leafy sea dragons, and watched a sea turtle slowly surface for air. They had fun.

Walking out of the aquarium with a bag full of the souvenirs Casey had insisted on buying her in the gift shop—a coffee mug and a T-shirt printed with the aquarium logo and a stuffed shark—Natalie was bemused that a day that had started so glumly had ended so pleasurably. The downtown area was beautiful, already wrapped in thousands of tiny LED lights that created a spectacular winter wonderland for the upcoming holidays. Trolleys ran from the aquarium all around the area on Christmas-light-viewing tours and even on a weeknight two weeks before Thanksgiving, business was already brisk.

She glanced at Casey and saw that he was watching her with an almost smug expression. Had he read her a little too well again? Was he privately taking credit for putting a smile on her face after catching her at a low point that morning?

She supposed she couldn't blame him, since it was entirely true.

"How about a walk along the river?" he asked, motioning toward the walkway that meandered alongside the gurgling Little Pigeon River.

Lined with benches and gazebos, the walkway was festooned with twinkling holiday lights overhead and was already being enjoyed by several couples. There couldn't be a more romantic setting for an after-dark stroll with a handsome man, and Natalie saw no reason at all to decline. "I'd like that."

It seemed only natural when Casey reached out to take her hand as they passed under an archway of lights on the bridge that led from the aquarium to the river walk. She laced her fingers comfortably with his, her souvenir bag dangling from her other hand as they walked so close together their shoulders touched. It was surprisingly easy to ignore the other people, the noises of the busy main street not far away, the problems that waited for her back at the cabin. Temptingly easy to concentrate entirely on the clear, cool night, the soothing sounds of rushing water, the pleasure of being so close to Casey.

"So, the aquarium was fun," Casey murmured in the companionable silence that had fallen between them.

"It was," she agreed quietly. "It's been a long time since I visited an aquarium."

"Sounds like it's been a long time since you've done a lot of things," he said a bit too casually.

"Maybe I've worked a little too hard the past few years," she admitted. "You know how it is."

"I know exactly how it is."

He seemed to wait for her to say something more, and she wondered if he was hoping she would tell more about herself. It was tempting. Casey really was a very good listener. But something held her back. Partially because she didn't want to ruin a nice evening with her depressing tale, and—even more significantly—because she didn't want him to know what had been said about her. She didn't want to watch his face when he mentally questioned whether there was any truth to the accusations.

"We really got a lot done today," Casey said after another brief pause. "A lot more than I expected when I thought it would be just me doing the work."

"I actually enjoyed it. It was such a nice day, and it feels good to do something to help Kyle and Uncle Mack. They were so generous to let me use the cabin."

"They were," Casey agreed. "But it's not as if they could rent it while it's being worked on."

"I know. But still…"

"I suspect your aunt and uncle would have let you use the cabin even if it was in top shape for rent," he said, glancing down at her with a smile. The twinkling lights reflected in his eyes, mesmerizing her. "They're obviously crazy about you."

She cleared her throat and tried to speak coherently. "I love them, too."

"I can tell. It's good to have family to turn to when you need them."

She wasn't sure if he was delicately fishing for information, but she didn't offer any, except to say, "It's nice that your father and his brothers and sisters stayed so close, unlike my dad and his other siblings."

"Actually, my dad and his twin were separated from their brothers and sisters for most of their childhood. There were seven of them altogether, and they were split up into the foster care system when their parents died. The oldest, my uncle Jared, was eleven. The youngest, Lindsey, was just a baby. My dad and his twin, Ryan, were seven. They didn't see each other again for twenty-four years."

Intrigued, Natalie paused to gaze up at his face in the pale light. "I hadn't heard about that. Molly hasn't mentioned it. Your family always sounds so close when the two of you talk about them."

He nodded. "They were reunited more than twenty-five years ago, and they've been pretty much inseparable ever since. All of them except Aunt Lindsey live around Dallas. She was adopted as an infant by a family in Arkansas and she's stayed close to them, but she comes to Texas often for Walker family gatherings."

Natalie was fascinated by the tale. She knew of other biological families that had been reunited after years of separation, but she'd never known any of them personally, not even once removed. "Were any of the others adopted?"

"Michelle was. She's the next youngest, just a toddler when her parents died. She was taken in by a very wealthy couple in Dallas. She was raised knowing she was adopted, but unaware that she had siblings. She found out after her adoptive mother died. She hired a private investigator, Tony D'Alessandro, to find her brothers and sisters. A few months later, she married the P.I. My uncle Tony, father of four of my cousins."

A P.I. It might have been a good time to mention that she, herself, was utilizing the services of a private investigator, but she pushed that fleeting thought to the back of her mind, focusing instead on Casey's story. "What about the other siblings? None of them were adopted?"

"No. Jared and Layla, the two oldest, were raised in foster homes until they were old enough to be out on their own. My dad and Ryan were placed together in a series of unsuccessful temporary homes, but they were…well, difficult, I guess you could say. They were angry about being separated from their family, naturally rebellious—"

"Imagine that," she murmured, thinking Casey must have inherited a bit of his father's temperament. After all, he had been one of the Walker family's "terrible trio."

He chuckled. "Yeah, I've been told I'm a bit like them. As are Aaron and Andrew. Anyway, my dad and his brother took off in their teens and bummed around on their own for years until they got wind that the sibs were looking for them. They came back to the fold on their own, before Tony and his team could locate them. They've been in Dallas since."

Doing some rapid math in her head, Natalie said, "You said there were seven siblings. You've only mentioned the fate of six. Did they never find the other one?"

"Miles died in a car wreck, several years before the others were reunited."

"Oh." She imagined how heartbroken they must have all been to hear that. "That's very sad."

"It was a blow for all of them," he agreed. "A few years later, though, they found out that he'd left a daughter behind. Brynn. She sort of stumbled into the family by accident, but that's a different story. Now she's a D'Alessandro as well as a Walker. She married Tony's younger brother Joe."

Natalie shook her head. "How do you keep up with all of this?"

He shrugged. "It's my family history. We've all heard the stories a million times."

"And Molly is… whose daughter?"

"Jared's. The oldest. He has a son, Shane, from a previous marriage."

"Families can certainly get complicated, can't they?" she mused, thinking of her own.

"You could say that." He glanced back toward the way they had come. "Ready to go back?"

She gave one last lingering glance to the light-bejeweled river and sighed lightly. "I suppose so."

He leaned over to steal a kiss before they started walking again. She offered her mouth freely, even eagerly. How could she resist in such a blatantly romantic setting?

Slipping an arm around her shoulders, he matched his steps to hers as they retraced their path. Mentally blaming it on the chill in the air, even though that had little to do with it, she nestled more closely into him.

Casey parked in front of Natalie's cabin, then turned to face her before opening the driver's door of his truck. Though it was fully dark outside, enough light filtered in from the security lamps for her to see that he was smiling as he looked at her in the shadows. "I had a great time."

"So did I."

"What are you going to do tomorrow?"

She gave a little shrug. "Read, maybe. Catch up on e-mail. Drive into town and pick up a few supplies."

"Are you sure you won't come with us?"

He had asked her during the drive back if she would like to join Molly and him the next day when they took Olivia to the amusement park. She had politely declined then, and she did so again now. "Thank you again, but I'm still going to pass. I think Olivia will enjoy having your complete attention, along with Molly's."

He looked as though he might argue a little more, but to her relief, he let it go. "I'll miss having you with us" was all he said.

"That's very nice of you."

"I wasn't being nice," he muttered, leaning toward her. "I mean it. I'll miss seeing you tomorrow."

Her gaze captured by his, she rested a hand on his chest. "I'll miss you, too. And I can't help being a little worried about that."

His mouth quirked upward into a wry smile. "Let me try to reassure you," he murmured, then kissed her before she could roll her eyes.

She slid her hand around his neck and returned the kiss. He gathered her closer, and she thought fleetingly that this would have been much more difficult in her car with a console between them. The bench seat of the truck gave them unimpeded access to each other—and Casey took full advantage of the opportunity. He shifted so that she would have had to sit in his lap to be any closer—and that was becoming a definite temptation as the kiss lingered and deepened.

He tilted his head to a new angle and kissed her again, his tongue teasing her, his teeth nipping lightly at her lower lip. As the kisses heated, so did the embrace. Hands wandered, explored, caressed. Their breathing grew rapid and ragged, and Natalie wondered if the heartbeat she heard thundering in her ears was hers, his, or a duet of both.

He finally pulled away with a low groan, shifting his weight on the plush seat as if he had suddenly become very uncomfortable. "It's been awhile since I've made out in a car," he muttered ruefully. "I won't lie, it's still fun…but maybe a bit more awkward than it used to be."

He could always make her smile, she thought as she had before—even when she shouldn't. Her hand wasn't quite steady when she brushed a tangle of hair away from her flushed-feeling face. "Maybe we should go inside," she suggested after only a momentary hesitation.

His eyes flared in the dim light, and she knew he was fully aware of what she meant. She had suddenly realized that she wasn't eager to go into that empty cabin alone, to spend another night tossing and turning and obsessing about her problems. Casey would definitely take her mind off anything else but him. And he didn't seem to mind being a pleasant distraction...

"I can't," he said with a sigh.

She blinked. "Um...you can't?"

He shook his head, and she didn't think she was imagining his regret, though he sounded definite. "I told Molly I would join them early. I guess I'd better get some sleep first."

Frowning, she searched his face. "That's a pretty lame excuse."

He sighed. "I know. I just...well, I don't want to rush into anything here. There are quite a few things you and I don't know about each other yet."

"I wasn't proposing a long-term relationship," she said shortly.

"I know. You're looking for a diversion," he said, repeating the term she had used before.

She shrugged. "That's all I can even consider at the moment. My life's in too much chaos right now to even think about anything more. But if you're not interested..."

He caught her arm when she shifted toward the door. "You know better than that."

She told herself that she would probably be relieved tomorrow that he'd declined her suggestion, but just then she was still irked. She really hated when someone made a decision on her behalf, "for her own good." Always had.

"I'd better go."

He trailed his fingers down her arm. "Okay if I call you tomorrow?"

Reminding herself that she was too old to pout, she nodded. "Yes, I suppose so. Don't bother walking me to the door," she added, when he reached for his door handle.

He dropped his hand. "Okay. I'll talk to you tomorrow then. Sleep well, Natalie."

Even as she closed the passenger door behind her, she suspected he knew exactly how unlikely it was that she would sleep at all well that evening. If there was any fairness in life, he would do some tossing and turning himself that night, she thought grumpily.

Chapter Eight

Natalie carried her coffee out to the deck the next morning. The air was a little cold, but she threw a jacket over her sweater and jeans and she was comfortable enough sitting in a rocker, sipping her coffee and looking out over the vista spread ahead of her. Low clouds shrouded the mountaintops, giving the illusion of gray smoke that had earned the range its name.

She had a long day ahead. She could do some research, hoping to discover something she hadn't found before on one of the many names on her suspect list. She could go to the grocery store and pick up supplies for the next few days. She could drive into Pigeon Forge and browse through some of the outlet stores, though she didn't need to spend a lot of money until she had another job lined up. Or...

She looked thoughtfully at the ladder still propped against the side of the cabin. Casey had said he was going to wash the cabin windows next. There was no reason at all she couldn't do that. It would take a while—the back wall of the cabin was almost all window to take advantage of the spectacular views. But it wasn't like any of her other options were any more appealing. And she could feel useful again.

In preparation for the chore, Casey had left a bucket with a telescoping squeegee and a reeled garden hose with a spray nozzle tucked beneath the deck. She gathered a couple of bath towels, a roll of paper towels and a bottle of detergent from inside, donned the driving gloves she had been using for work gloves and propped the ladder securely in front of the first window.

She had just set her foot on the bottom rung when she realized she was not alone. Looking down, she smiled. "Hello, Buddy."

The stray had materialized out of nowhere. Sitting only a few feet away from the ladder, he wagged his tail and gave her a doggie smile in return.

"I'll get your food and water."

He made a rumbly sound that was somewhere between a whine and a soft bark. It was the closest he'd come to making any noise around her, she realized.

He let her come very close to set the bowls on the ground. While she knelt nearby, he gulped down part of the kibble and lapped some water. And then he walked over to her and rested his head on her knee, gazing up at her with a soulful look that put a lump in her throat.

"You're welcome," she said huskily, patting his head. "You know, you could really use a bath. I don't suppose you'd let me wash you while I'm washing windows."

He wagged his tail against the ground and made another friendly sound that told her nothing about his openness to being bathed. Giving him another pat, she straightened. "I'm going to start washing windows now. If you decide you want me to wash you while I'm at it, let me know."

The dog sat near the base of the ladder when she went back up. She set the bucket of soapy water on the top shelf of the ladder and got to work, swabbing the glass of the nearest window with the telescoping squeegee. She didn't know if this was the most efficient way to do the job, but the windows would be clean when she finished.

She'd been working for well over an hour when she took her first break. Sitting on one of the steps leading up to the deck, she sipped from a bottle of water and eyed a few clouds gathering on the horizon.

"Looks like it could rain this evening," she commented to Buddy, who sat beside her, leaning against her leg. "Where do you take shelter when it rains, Buddy? Under a tree out there? That can't be fun."

The dog made that funny sound again, making her smile. "You know it's going to be winter very soon. The forecasters say this moderate weather's going to end in a few days. They're expecting some pretty low temperatures by the end of next week."

Buddy yawned.

"Yes, well, that's easy for you to say, but it gets cold here in the mountains in the winter. Snow, ice, freezing rain. Maybe you survived one season like that, but there's no guarantee you would survive another. You need a home."

He wagged his tail and lightly butted his head against her leg, hinting for her to rub his ears.

"I can't take a dog," she told him firmly. "I live in an apartment complex that only allows cats. I know that's rather discriminatory, but that's the way it is. So Casey's going to find you a home, okay? With a nice family who'll feed you and make sure you have a warm, dry place to stay when the weather turns bad."

Curling up on the ground beside the stairs, he rested his head on her leg and closed his eyes.

Suddenly feeling a bit foolish for engaging in a conversation with a dog, Natalie stood and went back to work.

She finished the windows by mid-afternoon. Tired and a little sore, she stood back to admire her work. She prepared to roll the hose back onto the wheeled metal reel, squeezing the spray nozzle first to empty any remaining water from the hose. To her amusement, the dog dashed forward to play in the spray. He'd seemed fascinated all afternoon by the water that had shot from the hose and splashed from the windows.

She let up on the nozzle and the spray stopped. Buddy turned to look at her expectantly, almost bouncing with eagerness.

"You want to play in the water?" she asked him.

He barked.

She turned on the spigot again and squeezed the nozzle, aiming a little lower this time. Buddy leaped into the spray, biting at the water as if trying to catch it. Natalie laughed, squeezing and releasing the nozzle to add to the game.

Inspiration suddenly struck and she set down the hose. "I'll be right back. Don't go anywhere."

The dog sat and watched as she dashed into the cabin. She was back only minutes later, this time carrying a bottle of baby shampoo and some more towels. Because she was prone to sties, she cleaned her eyelashes with baby shampoo every morning during her shower. She figured if it was gentle enough for her eyes, it would be the same for Buddy.

He was sitting right where she'd left him. She set the bath supplies near him and though he looked at them curiously, he didn't seem bothered by the sight of them. She pushed the sleeves of her sweater higher on her arms and picked up the hose. Buddy jumped to his feet, barking excitedly again.

She couldn't help laughing at his antics. Who'd have imagined that the skittish, elusive mutt Casey had first spotted only days earlier would turn into such a clown after a few good meals and a little attention?

The bath got her almost as wet as the dog, but he didn't try to resist her when she sprayed him down and rubbed shampoo into his medium-length hair. He actually seemed to enjoy the process, and she decided that he must have been someone's pet at one time. The bath process seemed familiar to him.

She should call the local animal shelter and ask if anyone had reported a lost pet matching Buddy's description. She should have done that already, she thought with a shake of her head. She blamed her distraction with her personal problems and her growing fascination with Casey for keeping her from thinking clearly about the stray dog.

She toweled him dry briskly, and he seemed to like that, too. He emerged from the towel grinning and panting. The bath must have made him hungry. As soon as he was reasonably dry, he trotted to his food bowl and began to munch on kibble.

Natalie stood back and watched him in amazement. He looked almost like a different dog. He was mostly reddish-brown with scattered white patches that were quite visible now that he was clean. Though she knew little about dog breeds, her stepfather owned a springer spaniel he called Monty. Buddy reminded her a little of Monty, though his coat wasn't quite as long. Maybe there was some springer spaniel in his mixed genetic makeup.

"Wait until Casey sees you," she said as she began to gather her supplies. "He's going to be so impressed."

Buddy wagged his tail, which was feathery now that it was clean. He could still use a good brushing, but she didn't own a dog brush and she had no intention of using her own good hair brushes on him. Her doggie altruism went only so far.

After stashing the window washing supplies where Casey had left them and making two trips inside to put away the things she'd brought out, she settled in a rocker again with a cup of hot tea. She needed to rest. She'd changed into dry clothes and donned a light jacket because the temperatures were falling as the sun set.

It would be dark within half an hour, she mused, looking at the purpling sky. It got dark so much earlier as winter approached. As he watched the light fade, her mood darkened as well. The mild euphoria left over from a day of productive hard work and playing with the dog leeched into a gloominess that matched the shadows creeping over the mountaintops toward the cabin.

As if sensing the change, Buddy rested his head on her knee and gazed sympathetically up at her. She hadn't even realized he'd come up onto the deck. She set her hand on his head, ruffling his soft, but still slightly matted ears.

Maybe there was something to the adage that pet owners were less prone to stress and depression, because having him there did make her feel a little better. Not that she intended to keep him, of course. It was just nice to have his company for now. Sort of like Casey, she thought with an attempt at humor that didn't particularly amuse her.

It must have been the thought of Casey's name that conjured him. "Wow," he said from where he stood at the bottom of the deck steps. "Where'd you get that handsome dog?"

Both Natalie and Buddy turned to look at him. Natalie, for one, certainly appreciated the view. Casey's hair was wind-tousled around his face and his bright eyes glittered in the sensor-activated security lighting that had just come on around the cabin. He wore an open-throated white shirt beneath his denim jacket, and dark, bootcut jeans with brown-and-tan, bowling-styled shoes. He looked like he'd just stepped out of a celebrity magazine, she thought with a slight sigh. One of those "most beautiful people" issues.

"Hi, Casey," she said, feeling her mood lighten even more.

Casey had been standing there for several minutes before he'd made his presence known. He suspected the dog had known he was there, but Buddy seemed totally focused on being petted by Natalie. Casey couldn't blame him for that.

"You gave him a bath?" he asked, amazed by how clean and soft the dog's formerly filthy coat looked now.

"Yes. I was washing windows and he loved playing in the water coming from the hose. One thing led to another, and now he's clean. He still needs to be brushed, but I didn't have anything to brush him with."

"I'll bring a dog brush tomorrow." Slowly climbing the stairs, he paused to glance at the shiny windows that now reflected the security lighting. "You washed the windows?"

"Yes. I had nothing else to do and it was such a nice day."

"You went up on that ladder?"

"Well, most of the way up. The telescoping squeegee thing helped me reach the really high parts."

He scowled, unable to block a mental image of her falling off the ladder and then lying hurt and alone for who knew how long. "That was awfully risky. What if you'd fallen?"

She shrugged. "I'd have sent Buddy for help, I guess. He's got Lassie's colors—maybe there's some collie mixed into his lineage."

Though he was still too unsettled by the thought to find much humor in her quip, he tried to smile anyway as he took a seat in the rocker beside hers. He doubted that she would appreciate him telling her that she shouldn't have been climbing ladders on her own, even though he still didn't think she should have taken the risk.

"I think it's safe to say there are several different breeds involved here," he said as Buddy walked over to greet him. He ruffled the dog's ears, appreciating the softness of the newly washed hair. "You sure look better, Buddy. Smell a lot better, too."

The dog made a low sound as if in agreement, then moved back to sit at Natalie's feet.

"Well, we know where his loyalties lie."

She shook her head in bemusement. "I don't know why. You're the one who started feeding him and talking to him."

"He has very discerning tastes."

"Yes, of course," she agreed drily. "I wasn't expecting you to drop by. I thought you said you were going to call."

"I was. But I wanted to see you."

She studied his face in the dim, artificial light. "Any particular reason?"

"Maybe I'm like Buddy," he replied lightly. "Drawn to you despite myself."

"I—um—how was your outing with Molly and Olivia?"

He laughed at her awkward transition, but went along for the moment to give her a chance to process what he'd said. "Actually it was Molly, Olivia and Riley."

"Riley?"

"Olivia's 'bestest friend' from preschool. Riley's a blue-eyed blond with a melting smile and an endless supply of energy. Combined with our own little redheaded dynamo, the activity level was very high today."

"Sounds like you and Molly had your hands full."

"Absolutely. The kids wanted to ride every ride in the kiddie part of the park at least twice, and begged to go on some of the rides for adults, even though they were too small to be admitted. They were absolutely fearless."

"Did you enjoy the day?"

"It was pleasant," he conceded. "I had fun watching the kids play. I'd like to go back with an adult sometime and see some of the music shows and craft demonstrations. The kids weren't particularly interested in that part of the park."

"I wouldn't really expect them to be at their age."

"No. By the way," he said, reaching into the inner pocket of his jacket, "I brought you something."

"You did?"

He nodded and tossed a small cellophane packet into her lap. "Taffy," he said. "They make it at the park. It's really good."

She smiled. "I love taffy. Thank you."

"I wanted to bring you a cotton candy cone, but it wouldn't fit in my pocket."

Smiling, she set the candy on the table between them. "Have you eaten?"

"We had an early dinner with the kids. Corn dogs and fries. Very healthy."

Her hesitation was barely noticeable before she asked, "I was just going to have a cup of herbal tea. Would you like to join me?"

"Yes," he said immediately. "I would. Thanks."

If she was surprised by his alacrity, she didn't let it show. She merely stood and moved toward the door.

Buddy followed right at her heels.

She stopped at the door, looking down at the dog. "Were you planning to go inside?"

Buddy wagged his tail.

Natalie looked at Casey, who shrugged as he stood just behind her and the dog. "Your call."

"I don't suppose he's housebroken."

"He could be. Now that we've gained his trust, he certainly acts like he's been a pet."

"And if he's not housebroken?"

"Then he's likely to act like a typical male dog and pee on everything in sight to mark his new territory."

"Great," she said with a sigh.

Buddy whined.

She melted, much to Casey's amusement. "Okay," she said to the dog, "you can come in. But I expect you to behave like a gentleman, understand?"

Buddy wagged his tail.

"I'll probably end up scrubbing the floors and the furniture," she muttered, opening the door into the kitchen. Buddy trotted in after her as if he'd been living there for years. Casey wasn't far behind.

Buddy sniffed around the living room and kitchen while Casey and Natalie watched, holding their breaths. And then, his exploration finished, Buddy curled up on a rug in front of the fireplace and put his head down on his paws. So far, he'd been a perfect guest. Casey hoped he remained that way.

"Would you like me to start a fire?" he called out to Natalie. "It would knock the chill off in here."

"That sounds nice," she answered from the kitchen.

A cubbyhole built into the bricks at the side of the fireplace held a dozen small fire logs. A basket beside the wrought-iron fire tools was filled with kindling. Casey fumbled around a bit, but had a small fire burning nicely by the time Natalie had the tea ready. Buddy gave a long sigh as the warmth penetrated to where he lay on the hearth rug.

"Better than the ground in the woods, hey, pal?" Casey murmured, giving the soft head a pat before rising.

Carrying the two mugs, Natalie joined him on the couch with a smile that made his heart trip over a couple of beats. Apparently she had forgiven him for the way they had parted the night before. It had taken him most of the restless night to forgive himself.

They sat on the couch, sipping tea and watching the flames while the dog dozed on the rug.

"Would you like to turn on the TV?" Natalie asked after several long, quiet minutes had passed.

"Not really." He was perfectly content to look at her and enjoy the peacefulness of the evening.

She nodded as if in approval of his choice. "Buddy looks settled in, doesn't he?"

"He does. I'm sure he's glad to be out of the cold."

"I put bowls of food and water in the laundry room for him."

"Are you going to let him stay inside tonight?"

She shrugged sheepishly. "I can't kick him back out in the cold. So far he's been well-behaved."

"Maybe he just hasn't had to relieve himself yet."

"Maybe," she admitted. "I guess he could sleep in the laundry room."

"Not sure how he would like being penned up in a little room after being free to roam."

"There is that," she admitted. "I suppose I could always put some blankets out on deck for him if he'd rather be outside."

Casey glanced at the blissfully content-looking dog and smiled.

Following his gaze, she said, "I realized today that we should probably contact the shelters, maybe the local newspaper, and see if anyone is missing a pet. It could be that he just got lost rather than abandoned. He might already have a home somewhere."

"That's possible. He's a nice dog. Handsome, too, now that he's clean."

"Yes, he's very sweet."

Setting down his cup of tea, Casey turned on the couch to face her. "Sounds as though you're getting attached."

She shook her head. "I'm not in a position to adopt a pet, no matter how sweet. I don't even know where I'll be living next month. It's best if I avoid any attachments for now."

Was there another message not so subtly hidden in her remarks? Probably, he answered himself. Natalie was making it very clear that she wasn't looking for commitment. Even when she had invited him in last night, she'd implied that she wasn't suggesting anything more than a night of fun.

He'd talked himself out of accepting last night because of a sudden concern that before they went any further with their relationship, temporary though it might be, they needed to talk. He should tell her what he really did for a living, and that he knew she too was an attorney.

Since then, he'd had second thoughts. She was, after all, the one who'd established the no-questions policy. Even if she hadn't actually put it in so many words, she'd managed to get the message across. Whatever made her leave her firm in Nashville, she didn't want to talk about it, didn't even seem to want to think about it, since she was working so hard staying busy with other things.

"I know the feeling," he sympathized. "I'm not looking for any commitments right now, either. Just not the right time. For a pet," he added.

She looked at him through her lashes, then asked, "So you think we'll be able to find a home for him?"

"I'm sure we will. But there's no hurry, is there? First we

have to see if anyone's reported him missing. And he's fine here in the meantime."

"He's welcome here, I guess," she said, keeping her tone nonchalant. "Though I'm not sure how much longer I'll be staying."

"When you need to leave, we'll make other arrangements."

"Okay. Fine." She looked at the dog again, her expression hard to read.

"The fire's going out," she murmured after a moment.

He glanced that way. "Do you want me to throw on another log?"

"No, it's fine. It's not really all that cold tonight. But I enjoyed watching the fire."

"I think Buddy liked it, too."

She smiled. "It certainly looks that way."

Perhaps sensing they were talking about him, Buddy raised his head, yawned, then stood and moved toward the sliding glass door. He paused there and looked over his shoulder at them with a brief bark.

"I believe he's saying he wants to go out," Casey commented, amused.

Natalie was already on her feet. She opened the door and Buddy trotted outside and down the deck steps.

"Do you think he'll come back in?" she asked Casey, who'd walked up behind her to see what the dog was going to do. "Or do you think he'll spend the night out in the woods again?"

"I don't know." He brushed a strand of hair away from her face, studying her grave expression. "Don't worry so much about it, Natalie. He's pretty good at taking care of himself."

"I know. I just, um, hate for him to get all dirty again," she prevaricated.

"I see."

She glanced up at him. "I know he'll be okay. And he'll probably be back tomorrow for more food."

He toyed with the ends of her hair around her face. "Very likely."

Her gaze locking with his, she bit her lower lip.

He touched her mouth with one finger, teasing her lips apart. "It would be a shame to leave marks here," he murmured, tracing her lower lip with his fingertip.

Her breath was warm and moist against his skin. A faint flush tinged her fair cheeks. He felt his own pulse beating in his temples as his body reacted to the nearness of hers. He wanted to tell her how beautiful she was, but he couldn't think of a way to do so without sounding trite or clichéd. He hoped she could see the sentiment in his eyes as he lowered his mouth toward hers.

A scratching on the door caught their attention just as their lips touched. A sharp bark followed the scratching, and both Natalie and Casey turned toward the door.

Buddy stood on his hind legs, his front paws propped on the glass as he barked at them again.

Casey glanced at Natalie with a faint smile. "I think you have your answer about where he wants to spend the night. And whether he's housebroken. That dog's been a house pet more recently than we thought."

She was already opening the door to let the dog in. "Don't think you're getting into my bed tonight," she said, and for a moment Casey blinked, then smiled sheepishly when he realized she was talking to the dog.

As for whether he, himself, would be getting into her bed—that remained to be seen.

Chapter Nine

Natalie found an old cotton blanket in the back of the linen closet and crumpled it into an inviting-looking pile in the laundry room beside the food and water bowls. Maybe Buddy would be content to sleep in there if she left the door open, though at the moment he was back on the hearth rug again, snoring gently.

Casey had returned to the couch. Like the dog, he seemed in no hurry to leave.

She could send him on his way. All it would take was a word from her and he would go. But she knew, as well, that one word was all it would take to convince him to stay. Whatever reservations he'd had last night seemed to be gone.

She took a moment to consider whether she had changed her own mind since last night. She pictured herself sending him away, closing the door behind him, spending another night thinking about him—or trying not to. And then she imagined what it might be like if he stayed.

The latter scenario was much more appealing.

"I made a bed for him, though it seems he prefers to stay right where he is," she said, sitting on the couch beside Casey.

"He does look content, doesn't he?"

"He must have just gotten lost. Who would have abandoned such a nice dog?"

"You'd be surprised at the stupid reasons I've heard. My mom's on the board of directors for an animal protection society in Dallas. She's become sort of a crusader during the past few years. While Buddy might have just wandered off and gotten lost, it's just as possible that he simply got bigger than his owners expected. He's a largish dog for an inside pet. I couldn't even keep him at my place in Dallas. Pets there have to be under twenty-five pounds, and Buddy's probably more like forty. Maybe someone had to move and didn't want to bother taking him along. Or got tired of feeding him and walking him and paying for his care… there are a lot of people who should never be trusted with animals."

It sounded as though he'd listened to more than a few speeches from his animal-activist mother.

"I guess we'll find out in the next few days if anyone's been looking for him."

"Maybe we will."

Something about the way Casey was looking at her told her he'd lost interest in talking about the dog for now. For that matter, so had she.

He reached out to toy with the ends of her hair, a habit he seemed to be getting into. Oddly enough, she rather liked it.

"I believe we were interrupted earlier," he murmured.

She smiled and leaned closer to him. "I think I remember where we left off."

"I was hoping you would."

A moment later she was in his arms.

For once, Natalie was entirely willing to just give herself up to the moment. She had been careful and sensible and practical and deliberate all her life—and look where it had gotten her. She was sure she would return to her old ways soon enough, but she was basically on vacation now. What else were vacations for, if not to get away from the stress of real life?

It was a rationalization she would never even have entertained only a few months earlier. But that was before her whole world had been turned upside down.

She'd been admiring Casey's appearance for days now. Since the first moment she'd seen him, actually. She'd thought his slightly shaggy, light brown hair was beautiful, with its rich texture and gleaming gold streaks. She appreciated it even more when she was able to bury her hands in it, feeling the softness, the thickness, the slight waviness of the strands surrounding her fingers.

She'd always been drawn to his eyes. So bright, such a compelling mixture of greens and blues. Gazing into them, she trailed a fingertip lightly over his lashes, envying him their length and thickness. It took two coats of mascara to get hers to look that long, she mused with a private smile.

Tracing the structure of his cheekbones and jawline, she decided that "clean" and "well-balanced" were the two terms that best described the lines of his face. If she'd had any artistic talent, she'd have loved to sculpt him, to try to recreate those lovely angles with clay or marble.

His shoulders were firm and straight, his abs well-developed, though not to the overworked, bodybuilder stage. He was slim and fit, but she suspected he maintained his condition through sports and other activities rather than regimented workouts at a gym.

He conducted his own explorations as they kissed and

caressed on the couch. His hands slid down her back, around her ribcage, up to her breasts. The kisses grew hotter, deeper, hungrier. Their breathing accelerated, roughened, and their movements grew more frenzied.

They were rapidly getting to the point of no return. Natalie's entire body was aching by the time Casey lifted his head to look down at her. She saw the question in his eyes even before he said huskily, "Natalie, I—"

A loud, shattering crash from the back of the cabin made both of them jump. Buddy jumped to his feet and barked toward the bedroom. After staring at Natalie for a blank moment, Casey pushed himself to his feet and ran toward the back. She followed a bit more slowly, still trying to clear her passion-dazed mind enough to understand what was going on.

The scene in the master bathroom made her stop abruptly in her tracks. Casey stood in the doorway, cursing angrily in a low voice. The large, new, beveled mirror that he had hung above the sink had fallen from the wall, smashing against the sink and countertop, raining shards of silvery glass everywhere in the bathroom.

The toiletry items she'd left sitting on the counter beside the sink were scattered, some of them broken from the impact. One of the bottles had held an expensive perfume. Now the bathroom reeked of what should have been a subtle floral scent.

"What on earth happened?" she asked, taking an instinctive step back from the overly aromatic mess.

"Isn't it obvious?" he asked irritably. "The mirror I hung last week fell off the wall. I guess I didn't use enough mastic or something. Whatever, I screwed it up."

She didn't take offense at his tone, since she realized he was angry with himself, not her. "Everyone makes mistakes, Casey."

"Yeah. I just make more than my share." Shaking his head in self-disgust, he said, "This is going to take a while to clean up. I'll have to go out to the truck to get my gloves. Don't go in, there's glass everywhere. Slivers as sharp as razors."

She nodded. "I'll get the broom and dustpan. And the large trash can to put the glass in."

"There's no need for you to help clean. This is my fault."

"It would take you hours by yourself. I'll help. I'll get my gloves."

"No. This glass would go right through those leather gloves you wear. Mine are thicker. I'll do the picking up. You can sweep, if you want, but you'd better put on thicker-soled shoes than those sneakers you're wearing now."

He was wearing sneakers, too, but the soles on his were thicker than hers. Nodding, she moved to the bedroom closet to pull out a pair of boots while Casey went out for his gloves.

He returned quickly, and was back in the bathroom doorway before she had gathered the cleaning supplies. His expression was grim when he looked over his shoulder at her. "You could have been standing there," he said, motioning toward the sink. "You could have been badly hurt, if not—"

"I wasn't standing there," she reminded him in a firmly calming voice. "There's no need to waste energy with what-ifs. It was an accident, that's all."

"It was incompetence," he disputed flatly. "I never should have tried to install that mirror on my own. I thought it was a simple job and I didn't realize—I'm no handyman, Natalie. I'm a—"

"Buddy, no." Natalie put a hand on the dog's head as he tried to crowd past her to see what Casey was up to. "You'll get glass in your feet in there. I'd better get him out of here before he gets hurt," she added to Casey.

Casey nodded and turned to start picking up the larger pieces of glass and dump them in the big plastic trash can she'd emptied and wheeled in for the job.

She ushered the dog back into the other room, slipped him a little meat from the fridge to bribe him into staying behind and went back into the bedroom, closing the door behind her.

The smell of the spilled perfume hit her as soon as she walked into the room. It must be giving Casey quite a headache, she thought.

She had already decided she would be sleeping on the couch that night. Considering the aromas wafting from the bathroom, she would likely dream of being lost in a botanical garden if she slept in the bedroom.

As for inviting Casey to stay with her…well, that moment had passed in a crash of glass and reality.

It took them more than an hour to complete the cleanup. They actually finished fifteen minutes earlier than that, but Casey obsessed about making sure not the tiniest sliver of glass remained to assault her unexpectedly. Making her cringe, he ran his bare hand over nearly every surface in the now-sparkling bathroom, so that if there had been a shard hidden somewhere it would have lodged in his palm. Despite her repeated assurances that she didn't blame him for the accident, he seemed to think he would deserve the pain if he did get punctured.

Reassured that the bathroom was glass-free, if still powerfully fragrant, he gathered his things. He paused long enough to pet the dog and praise him for being a good boy while they'd worked, and then he moved toward the door.

"I'll order a new mirror at my expense first thing in the morning," he assured Natalie. "And I want to repay you for anything that was broken in the crash. I'm sorry about the inconvenience."

She was getting tired of arguing with him. She merely nodded and opened the door for him, vowing to herself that she would just keep putting him off about the broken items until he forgot about them. She had no intention of taking his money for a few lost toiletries. She rarely wore perfume, anyway; the bottle had been a gift from Thad. Hardly a treasured memento.

He hesitated on the doorstep, as if he felt as though there was something more he needed to say, or do. And then he gave her a wry smile and murmured, "Good night, Natalie."

"Good night."

She closed the door behind him.

Turning to look at the dog sleeping by the fire, she sighed deeply. "Well, Buddy. Looks like it's just you and me tonight."

A low snore was his only response.

Shaking her head, she moved wearily toward the bedroom to retrieve a blanket and pillow. She wouldn't bother pulling out the bed from the sofa. There was plenty of room as it was, considering she would be sleeping alone.

It was almost eleven when Casey walked into his own cabin, his ego still stinging, his body still aching with frustration. He couldn't even think about sleeping yet. He knew he would lie in bed hearing the sound of that mirror crashing from the wall and picturing Natalie standing in front of it when it did. He shuddered.

What kind of hubris had made him think he could be a handyman with no training, no experience? Had he thought it was that easy compared to being an attorney? Had he really been that arrogant, so oblivious that it hadn't even occurred to him that a mistake on his part could cause more than simple property damage?

He really needed to tell Natalie the truth about himself. He'd started to do so tonight, but they'd been interrupted by Buddy and then he'd gotten too busy cleaning up the broken glass. Or so he'd told himself.

Maybe he would tell her tomorrow. It wasn't like it was a

big, dark secret. Without much interest, he glanced at the screen of his cell phone, noting that he'd missed calls that evening from his father, one of his aunts, his cousin Jason and his cousin Andrew. He'd silenced the ringer on his phone earlier. He hadn't wanted his evening with Natalie interrupted by calls.

It wasn't quite ten o'clock back in Dallas, not too late to return any of the calls. He should at least call his dad, he thought, gazing morosely down at the screen. The thing was, he just wasn't in the mood to talk. Everyone wanted to know when he'd be home, and he wasn't yet ready to answer that question.

He knew he needed to go back. The only thing holding him here was indecision.

And Natalie.

He knew he shouldn't be thinking that way. Knew very well that she wasn't looking for anything serious. He had tried not to let his emotions get involved with their…flirtation, for want of a better word. But he might as well admit it—he was falling hard for her.

The thought of saying goodbye to her, maybe never seeing her again—well, he just wasn't ready for that yet. Which meant he should probably start spending less time with her—but he didn't think he could do that, either. It had been ridiculous how much he had missed her while he'd been at the amusement park with Molly and the kids.

He could be headed for real trouble here, he thought with a frown. As if his life hadn't been complicated enough already.

Considering everything, Natalie slept fairly well on the couch. She woke a little sore from all the unaccustomed activity the day before, but she figured a hot shower would take care of that. She was relieved to discover that leaving the vent fan running all night had cured the master bath of the perfume overdose.

Buddy had spent the night on the hearth rug, ignoring the bed she'd made for him in the laundry room. She let him out while she made her coffee, watching through the window as he ran around the yard, sniffing and scratching. He seemed to enjoy being outside, but just as she was ready to go take her shower, he was back at the glass door, scratching for entrance.

He was certainly taking to the indoor life, she thought with a wry smile, moving to let him in.

"You stay here," she told him. "I'm going to get dressed. If the phone rings, take a message," she added, laughing a little as she moved toward the bedroom. She laughed again when Buddy yipped as if in agreement.

She took a hot, leisurely shower, dried her hair, applied a little makeup and then dressed in a soft red sweater and jeans. Ready for the day, she glanced at her watch. It was eight-thirty back in Nashville. That should be late enough on a weekday morning to make a business call, she decided, dialing Beecham's number. If she got his voice mail again, she intended to leave a very pointed message for him.

But Beecham answered in the same cheery, busy-sounding tone he always used with her. "Good morning, Ms. Lofton."

She didn't bother with trivialities this time. "Have you looked into the source of Cathy Linski's extra money? Have you found out anything new since the last time I talked to you?"

"I've been following some rumors about Miss Linski," he replied with a slightly condescending tone that set her teeth on edge. "She's been running with a pretty plush crowd lately. Lots of money flowing with that bunch."

"So I've heard. So where is she getting her money?" Natalie demanded impatiently. "She's not making that much at the firm. And as far as I know she hasn't come into any inheritances. Have there been any new media leaks about clients during the past couple of weeks? Anything that could account for Cathy's extra income?"

"I'm following some pretty good leads," he assured her.

"You've told me that before."

"I know, but these are real promising. Tell you what would help, if I had a little extra cash to grease the wheels, so to speak. You know, people like this are motivated by money."

Natalie stared at her phone in disbelief for a moment before putting it back to her ear. "You're asking me for more money?"

"Just a little cash advance," he assured her quickly. "Against the final payment."

"I've already paid you an advance. And I've gotten damn little in return for it," she snapped.

"Now, Ms. Lofton, I told you when you hired me that it could take a few weeks to get you all the proof you need. You told me it would be worth it, if it meant clearing your name."

"And it would be. But since I'm no closer to that now than I was when I hired you, I am not at all satisfied with your services."

"Just let me explain—"

"I don't want to hear any more explanations. I've done what you asked, Mr. Beecham. I've cleared out and left you to do your job, but I can't see that you've accomplished anything I couldn't do from here. I'm not giving you another cent until I see an itemized statement about what you've done on my behalf and a report about anything you've learned."

"Hey, we agreed—"

"We agreed that you would do a job. I'm going to require evidence that you've done what you advertised."

"But I—"

"I'll expect a call from you when you have the report ready," she said. "And I'll expect it soon. Good day, Mr. Beecham."

Her hands weren't quite steady when she snapped the phone

closed. It was a combination of anger, frustration and fear. Fear that she'd made a terrible mistake hiring this man. That she'd have to invest even more in someone else who might not produce any results. That she would never be able to prove that the accusations against her had been both unfounded and unfair.

Someone knocked on the back door, drawing her out of those unhappy thoughts. In the living room, Buddy barked, sounding excited. She knew just how he felt.

As she'd expected, Casey stood on the deck, looking at her through the glass. He gave her a little smile, and she smiled back, relieved that he seemed to be over his chagrin from last night. It was a measure of how besotted she was that she didn't at first notice Kyle standing beside him.

By the time she opened the door, she had her emotions under control. She hoped. "Good morning, Casey. And Kyle. Nice to see you."

"Thanks. I understand you had a little excitement last night."

Her mind went immediately to the wrong place, making her cheeks warm a bit before she said, "The mirror, you mean? Yes, it certainly startled us."

"I've already ordered another," Casey told her. "It should be here in a couple of days."

"I told him he didn't have to pay for the replacement," Kyle said with a shake of his head. "We've all made our share of mistakes, but he insisted on paying."

"Maybe the mirror was defective," Natalie suggested. "After all, it stayed in place for several days after Casey mounted it. Then it just fell for no reason."

"I didn't use enough glue," Casey corrected her. "It finally just gave way. But thanks for offering the excuse."

She shrugged.

"We're going to be working on the roof today," Kyle said,

changing the subject. "We thought we should warn you before we get started. I hope our pounding doesn't disturb you too much."

"Maybe I'll drive into town and visit my aunt."

Kyle chuckled. "Good idea."

Kyle was gone by the time Natalie returned to the cabin that afternoon. She had deliberately stayed away a good portion of the day, having a long visit with her aunt and then spending some time shopping and browsing through some of the quaint shops in town.

Seeing Casey's truck still parked in her driveway, she wondered if he was still working or if he was waiting for her to return. Maybe both.

Her arms full of packages, she walked toward the cabin. Casey appeared from around the corner, having heard her arrive. Buddy followed at his heels, bounding ahead to welcome Natalie home.

"Need some help?" Casey asked.

Gratefully, she offered one of the bags she'd been juggling. He took that one and another, lightening her load considerably. "Did a little shopping, huh?"

Though she thought it was obvious, she nodded. "A little."

"Did you have a nice visit with your aunt?"

"I did, thank you. How did the roofing job go?"

Following her into the cabin, he set the bags on the kitchen table. "Good. Kyle showed me how to fix shingles. I managed to hit my thumb with the hammer only once."

She winced when he showed her the bruised nail. "Ouch. That must have hurt."

"Let's just say Buddy might have learned a few new words."

She smiled and looked down at the dog, who was already settling on his hearth rug. "How did he do today?"

"Great. He just hung around the yard while we worked. Chased a couple of squirrels. Ate some kibble. Made friends with Kyle."

"You know, I think he's already gaining weight."

Casey nodded. "I think you're right. He's certainly been eating well the last few days."

"I placed a 'found dog' ad in the local paper. I gave some general information about him, but I think anyone who calls should give us more specific details. You know, just to make sure they're the real owners."

"Makes sense."

She shot him a look to see if he was making fun of her, but she couldn't read his expression.

Bustling around the kitchen, she put away the groceries she'd purchased. And then she opened another bag, looking at Casey from beneath her lashes as she pulled out a few things she'd picked up at the pet store.

"You've been shopping for Buddy," Casey commented, watching her.

"Just a few things," she said offhandedly. "The stainless steel bowls will be easier to clean than the plastic margarine tubs. The treats are good for his teeth. They control tartar."

"And this?" He picked up a brightly colored, hard rubber ball covered with knobs.

"Exercise," she replied. "The clerk at the pet store said lots of dogs Buddy's size enjoy playing with these."

Setting the ball back on the table, Casey said, "I brought a dog brush with me today. Brushed him out during a break this afternoon. Did you notice?"

She was a bit chagrined that she had not. It meant she'd been all too focused on Casey himself. "He looks great," she said, choosing not to directly answer the question. "Did he like being brushed?"

"He seemed to enjoy it. Except when I snagged a tangle. Even then he only flinched. Never gave me any trouble."

"Good."

She filled the new bowls with food and water and set them in the laundry room in place of the plastic tubs.

"So tomorrow you're putting in the hot tub?" she asked, feeling a sudden urge to fill the quiet with chatter, and busied herself by making tea.

"Yeah, that's the plan. It's supposed to be delivered and wired at ten o'clock. Kyle and I will be doing some carpentry work around it. He's already reinforced that end of the deck in preparation for the tub, but he wants to build a bench there to sit on and to keep towels and robes handy."

"Will the tub be open all winter?"

"It will be heated and ready, yes. Kyle said it comes with a cover that's pretty easy to take off and put back on. They have to schedule regular cleanings and chemical treatments. Apparently, it's a bit of trouble, but if it helps them keep the place rented, I guess it's worth it. The competition's pretty brisk. There are a lot of vacation cabins around here, some of them pretty luxurious."

"I'm sure there are other people like me who prefer a more simple retreat."

"That's what keeps your uncle and Kyle in business," he agreed. "Anyway, you should be able to try the spa yourself by Saturday. Sunday at the latest. You'll be here through the weekend, won't you?"

"Yes. Aunt Jewel said the cabin is available for two more weeks, though I'm not sure I'll be here that long. How about you?" she asked, trying to sound as casual as he had.

"My cabin's available for another ten days. They have reservations beginning a week from Sunday. They're having a new metal roof put on this week, which is the only thing left to be done to it."

She studied his face as he pushed a hand through his hair. "You look a little tired."

He shrugged. "I must have gone up and down that ladder a couple dozen times today. Roofing's a hard job, and all we were doing was repair work."

"I suppose all construction work is physically demanding."

"No kidding. I've found some muscle groups I didn't know I had. And all of them have been sore at some point during the past couple weeks." He took a sip of his tea, then added, "I guess it's a good thing I have a white-collar job. Considering the assorted cuts and bruises I've accumulated so far, I could seriously hurt myself if I keep this up much longer."

He was probably trying to make her smile, but her attention had been captured by his reference to his "white-collar job." She tried to speak as lightly as he had, "Um, yes, I believe I've commented on your accident-proneness."

"Once or twice. The good thing about living in a condo back in Dallas is that there's a maintenance crew to deal with the repairs and upkeep."

She didn't know if he was just making small talk or deliberately dropping hints about his life back in Dallas in an attempt to open himself to questions. "You live in a condo?" she said, nibbling at the bait.

"Yeah. It's in a high-rise in downtown Dallas, close to the law firm where I work. You can see why I've enjoyed being here in the peace and quiet of the mountains for the past few weeks. It's a nice change from all the traffic and the crowds and the grind."

Her fingers felt as though they'd just gone numb. Very carefully, she set her teacup down on the counter. "You're a... you're an attorney?"

"Yeah. You didn't really think I was a professional maintenance man, did you?"

"No. I didn't think that."

She clasped her hands in front of her in an attempt to hide the trembling she wouldn't have wanted to try to explain. "So, you're on vacation?"

"A leave of absence," he said with a slight shrug. "I was getting a little too close to burning out after a challenging year, so I took some time off. I suppose I'll have to get back to my real work soon."

"You can't have been out of law school for long."

"A couple of years. I skipped a couple years of elementary school, took some college classes during high school, earned my bachelor's degree when I was twenty. All of which got me into my career sooner, but might have led to some of the burnout."

"I can see why. You must have worked very hard."

"For some reason it seemed important to rush through everything. Now I'm wondering why I did. I guess it's that overachiever gene my parents passed down. Dad's a senior partner in a security firm with his brothers, Mom's CEO of an accounting firm, my maternal granddad was one of the most prominent prosecuting attorneys in Chicago for many years. Slacking off was not allowed."

He had some serious connections. That probably explained why he'd been at liberty to take this much time off so early in his career. He would probably be a junior partner by the time he was her age.

How could she tell him why she was no longer employed by her own firm?

She knew there was probably more to his leave of absence than a close brush with burnout. Surely there had been some catalyst that had driven him here. Some reason behind the haunted expressions she had occasionally spotted on his face when he thought she wasn't looking. But whatever it was, she couldn't imagine it was as bad as being accused of betraying client confidentiality for monetary gain.

She would bet everything she had left in savings that Casey Walker was a scrupulously ethical attorney. Would he believe her when she said that she had always tried to conduct herself the same way? Or would he be more inclined to remember the old adage about smoke surely indicating fire?

"You look so serious," he murmured, brushing her hair back from her face. "I won't ask what you're thinking, but if you want to share, I'm always available to listen."

She couldn't meet his eyes. With a long, low sigh, she murmured, "I wouldn't know how to begin."

"Begin wherever you like. Whatever it is, Natalie, I'd like to help you, if I can. I hate seeing you so sad."

Very slowly, she lifted her gaze to his face. He was looking at her with such concern that it made her throat ache. She could almost believe that he truly cared about her when he looked at her this way. And that was a dangerous way to think. She'd been hurt too much lately by people she'd thought had cared about her.

Casey lowered his head to brush a kiss over her lips. And then he drew back just far enough to speak, his forehead resting lightly against hers. "I think I should tell you—"

The cell phone clipped to his belt rang loudly, a sharp, intrusive tone that demanded his attention. Both of them jumped, and Buddy lifted his head off the hearth rug, as startled as they were by the sudden disruption of the quiet.

Muttering a curse, Casey glanced at the screen. "It's my dad. I'll call him back later—"

"No. Take the call. I'll see what we have for dinner."

She all but pushed him into the living room on the pretext of giving him privacy for the call. She needed that distance, needed a few moments to gather herself and come to terms with the things Casey had just told her about himself.

Gripping the kitchen counter, she thought of how ironic it was that Casey's personal revelation had served only to drive them further apart rather than drawing them closer together.

She sent Casey away a short time later, claiming that she had several phone calls of her own to make. "I haven't talked to either of my parents in a few days, and I need to call them both," she said. "My chats with Mom usually last quite a while, and I'm sure you'd be bored."

Looking as though he would have liked to argue with that, he merely shrugged and allowed himself to be hustled to the door. "I'll see you tomorrow," he said from the open doorway. "Maybe we'll have more opportunity to talk then."

"Yes, maybe we will," she replied lightly, though she wasn't sure she'd be any more ready to talk about her mortifying situation the next day. "Good night, Casey."

He caught her chin and brushed a kiss over her lips. "Good night, Natalie. Sleep well."

Closing the door behind him, she placed a trembling hand on her mouth. Sleep well? She sincerely doubted that she would.

Chapter Ten

When someone knocked on the front door late the next morning, Natalie assumed it was Casey. Automatically smoothing her hair, she moved to open it, bracing herself for a difficult conversation. Sometime during her restless night, she had decided she might as well tell Casey the whole, embarrassing truth about herself.

She and Casey had become friends during the past days, if nothing more. He had been kind to her, providing more than the pleasant distraction she had first contemplated with him. He'd been thoughtful and entertaining, making her smile more than she had in a long time. And he had been honest with her, if a bit belatedly. She owed him the same in return.

With that little pep talk in mind, she opened the door, then blinked in surprise when she found Rand Beecham there instead of Casey. The attractive-in-a-burly-ex-cop-sort-of-way P.I. gave her his studiedly charming smile and greeted her cheerfully. "Good morning, Ms. Lofton. I hope I'm not disturbing you."

"How did you find me?" she asked, surprise making her a little stupid.

He merely laughed. Motioning with the manila envelope he held in one hand, he asked, "May I come in? I have the information you requested."

"You've found out who was responsible for the leaks from the firm?" she asked eagerly.

"Well, no, not conclusively," he replied, easing past her into the cabin. "I haven't had a chance to do anything more since we talked yesterday. But you wanted to see an accounting of what I've done for you, correct?"

She frowned and closed the door. Seeing a stranger, Buddy abandoned his hearth rug and slunk into the laundry room where his food and water bowls sat. Apparently there was something about Beecham he didn't like. Natalie completely understood. "You could have e-mailed the report. You've wasted a long drive here when you could have been working on my behalf."

"And as I told you yesterday, I need another advance before I can go any further," he argued smoothly. "It's not that I don't trust you to pay me at the end of the job," he added, his tone a bit too pointed now, "but this is standard operating procedure, Ms. Lofton."

She held out her hand. "Let me see your report."

"Absolutely."

Being an attorney, she knew all about billable hours. She knew how to record them, how to justify them, even how to manipulate them if necessary, though she had always tried to be scrupulous in recording her time. Still, Rand Beecham's report was a study in creative billing. According to his time records and hourly charges, he had already earned everything she had given him as an advance and more. While she knew that effort did not always equal result, the very short, not particularly informative summary at the end of his report did not satisfy her at all that he'd been worth the investment.

"This tells me nothing I didn't find out on my own through telephone gossip," she said in dissatisfaction.

"Oh? Did you know that Cathy Linski has just put a down payment down on a nice West End condo?"

"A condo in West End?" Natalie repeated blankly. "You're kidding."

"So you *didn't* know."

Brushing off his smug tone, she shook her head. "No. And there's no way she can afford a place like that. Not on her clerical salary at the firm."

"Exactly."

"I don't know," she murmured. "I can't imagine she'd have made that much with those few leaks that were attributed to me. I mean, sure, it was juicy gossip and the tabloids had a field day with it all—but would they really have paid her enough to finance an entire new lifestyle?"

"Perhaps. Especially if she's agreed to provide more fodder once the higher-ups in the firm relax. If they're satisfied that you were behind the leaks, they might consider the matter closed and let their guard down, giving Ms. Linski access to some of the confidential files again."

There was still something that just didn't feel right about that scenario, Natalie thought uncomfortably. "Is this the only lead you have? The fact that Cathy is buying a condo?"

"I found that, I can find more," he assured her. "If her money's coming from one or more of the tabloids, I'll find the proof. It's just going to take a little more time."

Which meant even more billing hours, she thought with a slight wince. She had managed to put some money into savings after paying off her student loans, but it wouldn't take long before that was gone if this investigation continued much longer.

"Maybe I should come back to Nashville, follow Cathy around myself, for a while," she mused aloud. "Maybe I can figure out what's going on with her."

"And get yourself slapped with a harassment suit? A restraining order, maybe? Remember, I'm a pro at this. I know how to follow her without her ever suspecting a thing. Give me a few more days, and I'll have everything you need."

He kept saying that, and she kept feeling like an idiot for believing him. But what other choice did she have? And besides, he *had* found an interesting lead about Cathy.

"Okay," she said with a sigh, mentally conceding that she was no private investigator. She'd probably be worse at that than Casey was at maintenance, she thought with a grimace. "I'll give you another five hundred dollars. But that's all, until I see more valuable results."

"Make it a thousand, as an advance against the final payment. I'll need a little extra for an assistant."

She swallowed hard and then nodded. "I'll get my checkbook," she said, turning toward the bedroom.

"Nice place," he called after her. "It's not so bad to have a vacation in a cozy mountain cabin while I take care of business back home for you, is it?"

"I'm not accustomed to anyone taking care of my business for me," she said as she rejoined him.

"That's what I do," he replied with a shrug. "So I'd advise you to enjoy your time here, do a little shopping, some sightseeing, take in a show. If there's any evidence to be found to clear your name, I'll find it."

"*If?*" she repeated with a frown, reluctantly handing him the check.

"If it exists, I'll find it," he repeated, and something about the way he looked at her as he tucked the check in his pocket made her blood pressure rise.

She didn't like the implication that there might be no evidence because she wasn't as innocent as she claimed. But if that were true, why on earth would she waste all this money hiring him to find that evidence? she asked herself in exasperation. More likely, he was just giving himself an out in case he failed.

And if that happened...well, she supposed she'd better be coming up with a Plan B, just in case.

Casey parked in front of Natalie's cabin just as the front door opened and a man walked out. He glanced at his watch, noting that it was before noon. Who was this guy, and why was he here this early in the day?

He reminded himself that it was none of his business who was visiting Natalie or why. But that didn't stop him from glaring at the guy as he strolled past the truck and climbed into a dark sedan.

Cop, Casey thought immediately. Or ex-cop. There was just something about the walk that he recognized. Was he a friend of Natalie's? More than a friend? Someone working for her? Or someone interrogating her?

There were too many possibilities for him to guess the answer. So he could either ask her outright or maybe she'd volunteer the information to satisfy his curiosity. Since she hadn't told him much of anything about herself thus far, he didn't have a great deal of hope for the latter. He'd given her the perfect opportunity to open up to him when he'd told her yesterday he was an attorney. She could have admitted then that she was also trained in the law. She hadn't. Instead, she'd drawn into herself and sent him on his way.

He was beginning to wonder if he would ever really know Natalie Lofton. He wasn't sure why he seemed so determined to try.

She must have seen him drive up when she'd let the other guy out. She waited on the porch for him. "Good morning," she said. "Where's Kyle?"

"He'll be here later. He had some other things to do first."

"Oh. Is there anything I can do to help you?"

"I'm just going to start taking down the deck railing, since we're putting up all new railing with built-in benches once the hot tub's installed."

"I'll get my gloves," she said, turning away from him. "I feel like doing some demolition today."

Apparently she wasn't going to even mention the guy who'd just left, Casey thought broodingly. And even though he reminded himself again that it was none of his business, it rankled him. Maybe he was still more sensitive about secrets and sneaking around than he had realized after the way his relationship with Tamara had ended.

If so, he needed to keep in mind that he and Natalie had no ties between them, nothing more than a holiday flirtation. She owed him no explanations, no confidences. So it made no sense that her silence hurt him.

And yet…it did.

The hot tub was installed by mid-afternoon on Saturday. Working side by side, Casey and Kyle had made great headway on the deck improvements. It helped that Kyle had brought a pneumatic hammer for this job, Casey thought, driving a nail into a redwood board with a loud pop of compressed air.

The tub looked good tucked into one corner of the deck. He'd been concerned that it would overpower the simple decor, but it fit right in, the blue liner encased in a redwood frame and accessed by two steps. He could imagine himself sitting in that bubbling spa—with Natalie, of course—sipping wine and admiring the view.

Speaking of Natalie…

He glanced toward the cabin doors. She'd been holed up in there all day, barely even looking out to check on the progress of the work on the deck. Buddy had been in there with her most of the time, coming out only to relieve himself and spend a few minutes being petted before heading back inside. Almost as if the dog thought Natalie needed him in there.

Casey sighed somewhat wistfully, wondering if he had made a tactical error in telling Natalie about himself. He had thought she deserved to know the truth about him, and he'd hoped the information would encourage her to open up to him. Instead, she had reverted to a distant acquaintance, making small talk with him, even working alongside him without any semblance of intimacy between them. There hadn't even been a goodnight kiss since he'd told her he was an attorney back in Dallas. And she still hadn't told him the identity of her visitor yesterday morning.

She finally appeared late that afternoon. She'd let Buddy out and she wandered out behind him, studying the spa while Buddy trotted down the steps and into the yard. "It looks nice," she said, walking slowly around the tub. "I'm sure this will be a popular feature."

"That's the hope." A little sweaty from the hard work he'd done that day, he pushed a hand through his hair. "We filled it and added the chemicals, so it will be ready to use tomorrow. Kyle said you should definitely try it out and let him know how you like it."

"Where is Kyle?"

"He got a call from one of the other rentals. Apparently someone's toddler flushed a toy down the toilet and now they have a plumbing crisis."

Natalie grimaced. "That can't be fun."

"No. Part of the job of being a property manager, though."

She put her hands into the pockets of the jacket she wore over her sweater and jeans. "It's getting chilly."

"Yeah. The forecasters are predicting rain later tonight."

"Yes, I heard."

They were actually talking about the weather. And wasn't that depressing?

He moved closer to her, looking down into her face. The urge to kiss her was so strong that it was all he could do to keep any distance between them. His voice was husky when he said, "Natalie—"

She gazed up at him, her lips parting just a little.

He cupped her face in his hands. "I wish you would—"

"Casey? Hey, Case, you here?"

The call from the other side of the cabin made him drop his hands with a frown. "That's weird. That sounded like—"

Craning her neck, Natalie asked, "Like who?"

Casey released a little sigh as two tall, dark-haired men rounded the side of the cabin, calling his name. "Like my cousin Aaron," he said. "Looks like you're about to meet the rest of the terrible trio."

Despite their identical faces, friends and family could instantly tell the Walker twins apart, something they had achieved deliberately. Andrew wore his almost-black hair very short, almost military in style. He favored dark clothing, grays and blacks and dark denim, and black boots. Aaron had allowed his hair to grow longer, so that it waved slightly around his face and on the back of his neck. He dressed more casually than his twin, choosing brighter colors and trendier styles.

Casey had heard some girls insist that Aaron was the better-looking twin, even though there was no discernable difference in their facial structure, only their personal styles.

"What the hell are you two doing here?" he demanded, staring at them with narrowed eyes.

"We came to bring you home," Aaron answered cheerily. "We decided you've played handyman long enough. We also figured that Kyle would thank us for preventing you from doing any real damage."

"Kyle told us where to find you," Andrew added, glancing from Casey to Natalie and back. "He said you had kind of a mess here from installing the spa and that you could probably use some help cleaning up."

"Looks like you've got most of it under control," Aaron said, glancing around. "The spa looks great."

Remembering his manners, Casey moved forward. "Guys, this is Natalie Lofton. Natalie, my cousins, Aaron and Andrew Walker."

He pointed to each of them as he said the names. He could tell by the way she looked at each of the twins that she was noting their differences and would remember. "It's very nice to meet you both," she said.

Andrew nodded. "Good to meet you, too."

"Pleasure to make your acquaintance," Aaron said, speaking over his brother.

Both of them studied her rather closely, and Casey suspected they were making her feel a bit like a zoo exhibit. She cleared her throat and said, "I need to get back to my laundry. Can I get any of you anything?"

They all assured her that they were fine. Excusing herself with a pleasant, if somewhat distant smile, she went inside, leaving Casey with his cousins. Buddy stayed outside, moving between Andrew and Aaron to be petted by them.

Casey waited until the door had closed behind Natalie before he spoke. "Seriously?" he demanded. "You've really come here to nag me about going back to Dallas? Don't you two have lives of your own?"

"Before you start chewing on us, you might ask yourself if you'd rather your mother had come instead," Andrew said evenly.

"My mother?"

Looking up from scratching Buddy's ears, Aaron nodded. "She was threatening. Your dad keeps telling her you're fine, but Aunt Lauren is convinced you're having some sort of breakdown and you need help. When Andrew and I volunteered to come in her place, she agreed to stay behind."

"Oh." Suddenly it didn't seem so bad to have his cousins there. "Well... thanks, I guess. But really, I'm okay."

"Looked like you're more than okay to me," Aaron murmured, glancing at the door through which Natalie had disappeared. "She's pretty."

"Listen, it's almost dark. If you guys really came up here to help, grab some of this stuff and throw it in the back of my truck. I'm sticking the extra pieces of wood in this box, and then I've got to sweep up."

The twins exchanged a look. "You actually want us to work?" Aaron asked.

Casey punched his cousin's arm. "Pick up the toolbox."

"Ow." But Aaron sighed and picked up the toolbox while Andrew started throwing wood into the box of scraps.

Natalie had known who the twins were the minute they'd rounded the corner of the cabin looking for Casey. She had seen from Casey's expression that he hadn't been expecting them.

Remembering Aaron's announcement that they were here to bring Casey home, she sighed, figuring her time with Casey was coming to an end. Which had been inevitable from the start, she reminded herself…but it still felt too soon.

Mentally replaying her first sight of the twins, she shook her head in bemusement. With their almost black hair and equally dark eyes, they were striking in both their similarities and their stunning good looks. Casey was a very good-looking man, but those two were freaking gorgeous. The fact that she still found Casey the more appealing of the three was an indication of how mesmerized she was by him. And maybe how badly she was going to miss him after he left.

She didn't want to think about that right now.

Though she'd used it as an excuse to escape the curious looks from Casey's cousins, she really had been doing laundry that afternoon. She had left a load of jeans in the aging dryer and since she no longer heard the machine running, she assumed the timer had buzzed while she was outside with Casey. She opened the door, only to be met by the sight of a mound of wet jeans.

Sighing in exasperation, she decided she must have forgotten to turn on the machine, though she would have sworn she remembered doing so. Closing the door again, she set the timer and pushed the start button. The dryer made a humming noise, but without the rhythmic thumping that would indicate that the drum was turning.

"Well, darn," she muttered.

She glanced toward the back door and sighed again. She would have to tell Casey about the problem. Whether he could fix it was another question.

She opened the door to find Andrew sweeping up the last of the sawdust from the deck. "Um—where's Casey?" she asked.

Leaning casually on the broom, Andrew replied, "He and Aaron carried some stuff to the truck. He should be—oh, here he is."

With Buddy right at his heels, Casey rounded the side of the house and started up the steps to the deck. "Are you looking for me?" he asked Natalie.

"Yes. I— Something's wrong with the clothes dryer. The drum isn't turning."

"Yeah? Okay, I'll come in and look at it."

Aaron laughed. "You think looking at it is going to make it work again? What do you know about fixing a clothes dryer?"

Casey lifted his chin and replied with aggrieved dignity, "There's a chance I can figure out what's wrong with it."

"A very slim chance," Aaron murmured.

Andrew stepped in before his cousin and brother could exchange any further barbs. "Actually, I helped dad work on mom's dryer once. Maybe I can help you figure it out."

Casey nodded. "Yeah, okay. Thanks for the offer."

"I'll help, too," Aaron said, following them toward the open doorway where Natalie still stood.

"Oh, yeah, I'm sure you'll be tons of help," Casey drawled sarcastically, as Natalie backed up to let the men in.

"I'll provide comic relief," Aaron quipped, winking at Natalie. "Although I imagine watching you guys pretending to be handymen will be funny enough."

Natalie couldn't help but return his smile. It was hard not to respond to Aaron's irrepressible charisma. Casey shot her a look over his shoulder that she couldn't quite interpret. Surely he wasn't checking out her response to his cousin's apparently habitual flirting?

She took her wet jeans out of the dryer, piling them into a

plastic basket. And then she and Buddy moved into the living room while Casey and the twins tore into the dryer. To give herself something to do, she checked her e-mail—what little there was of it. She had heard nothing more from Beecham since he'd left yesterday, so she had no idea if he was making any more headway on her case. She suspected he had not.

An interesting cacophony of sounds came from the laundry room. Thumps, squeaks, creaks, hammering. Curses—from Casey—and laughter—mostly Aaron's—interspersed with calm instructions—Andrew's. After perhaps half an hour, all three came out in the living room, grinning like warriors who had just won a skirmish.

Lifting an eyebrow in Casey's direction, she asked, "You fixed it?"

"Yep."

Andrew cleared his throat rather loudly.

"Okay, we fixed it," Casey confessed. "But I could have managed that one on my own," he added in Andrew's direction. "Anyone could have seen that the belt had just slipped off the drum."

"I expected to find that the belt had broken," Andrew said. "That's what happens more commonly. It's rare to find that it's just slipped off instead."

"You can dry your jeans now," Casey told Natalie. "The dryer should work just fine."

"Thank you. Thank you all," she added, glancing at his cousins.

"It was nothing," Aaron assured her with a smile.

Both Casey and Andrew scoffed at that.

"It was nothing for you, you mean," Casey accused. "You didn't do anything."

"I held the flashlight."

Shaking his head, Casey turned back to Natalie. "These miscreants and I are going to a little Mexican place downtown for dinner. Molly said it's pretty good. Would you like to join us?"

"Yes, please come, Natalie," Aaron seconded with a smile. "I'd appreciate having an intelligent conversation with someone during dinner, something I certainly won't get from these two."

She smiled back, but shook her head. "Thank you, but I have some calls to make this evening. I'm sure the three of you have a lot to catch up on."

Telling them he would join them in a few minutes, Casey sent his cousins outside. Exchanging "Good nights" with them, Natalie noticed that Andrew, especially, looked at her a bit longer than necessary as he moved toward the door. As if he were studying her face, looking for…what? Whatever it was, his scrutiny made her uncomfortable, as if he were seeing more in her expression than she wanted him to know about her.

Casey gazed down at her when they were alone. "Are you sure you won't come with us? My cousins will be on their best behavior. Mostly."

"No, not tonight, thanks."

He put a hand to the back of his neck and squeezed, his expression somber. "We were going to talk before they showed up to interrupt us. There are still some things I think you and I should clear up."

She knew he was right, but now wasn't the time. Not while his cousins were waiting outside for him. "We'll talk later. You'd better go. They're waiting for you."

Nodding, he reached out to rest a hand on her shoulder. "I'll be thinking about you tonight," he murmured. "I seem to be doing that a lot lately."

A little sigh escaped her before she could stop it. "I've been thinking about you a lot, too," she admitted. "Too much, I'm afraid. There are things…well, this isn't a good time for me."

"I know," he murmured. "Me, either. But that hasn't seemed to stop me from wanting to be with you."

She gazed up at him, moistening her lips as she tried to think of something to say.

He cupped her face in one hand and leaned over to brush a kiss across her lips. "We'll talk more tomorrow. Good night, Natalie."

She barely resisted an impulse to grab hold of him and give him a kiss that would make the spicy Mexican food he planned to eat later seem tame in comparison. After he'd let himself out, she sank onto the couch, wishing she had given in to that particular urge.

Chapter Eleven

Because he was so dirty from the manual labor he'd done that day, Casey insisted on returning to the cabin where he'd been staying so he could clean up before dinner. His cousins followed him inside, carrying the bags they'd brought with them from Dallas, since they intended to spend the night in the A frame.

"There's only one bedroom," Casey warned them, tossing his jacket over the back of a chair. "You'll have to crash on the couch and the floor."

"We'll arm wrestle for spots later," Andrew said with a shrug, tossing his bag next to the couch.

"So, you've been spending a lot of time with Natalie, huh?" Aaron asked as Casey starting emptying his pockets on the breakfast bar that separated the kitchen from the living room.

Casey looked up warily. "I've been working on her cabin. You know that."

"Yeah, but I got the distinct impression her cabin's not all you've been working on, if you know what I mean."

Casey scowled and threw his wallet on the bar. "Don't," he warned his cousin curtly.

Wearing his most innocent expression, Aaron shrugged. "Just saying. It's…interesting that you would meet up with another lawyer while you're on your leave of absence, isn't it?"

His hands on his hips, Casey narrowed his eyes. "How did you know she's a lawyer?"

"Molly might have mentioned it over the phone a couple of days ago. She said Natalie was with a big firm, but she's looking for another job now."

"What makes you think that's anyone's business but hers? And why was Molly gossiping about Natalie to you?"

"She didn't tell me much. Only that Natalie's an attorney from Nashville who's been spending some time here. Hiding out."

"She isn't hiding out," Casey snapped, annoyed that Aaron had just summed up more than Casey had learned from Natalie herself. "She's just taking some time off. The same thing I'm doing, remember?"

"Yeah, well, there's a little more to it than that where Natalie's concerned."

Something about Aaron's tone made Casey's blood heat. He spun toward Andrew. "You didn't."

Andrew grimaced. "I told Aaron you wouldn't like the fact that we've been asking questions about her."

"But you did it, anyway?"

"Look at it this way, Case," Aaron said. "You meet a woman who won't tell you what she did for a living or why she's not doing it anymore. You get so involved with her that you don't want to come home, and you seem to stop worrying about your own job. That's enough to make us a little concerned. Molly said you've been spending almost all your time with Natalie."

"Sounds like Molly's been saying too damned much."

"You know how her mouth gets away from her sometimes. And maybe I sort of let her believe you'd been talking to me and I already knew some of that."

Casey turned again to Andrew. "You've been encouraging him in this?"

Andrew didn't even look guilty when he shrugged. "You really don't know much about her, do you?"

Sighing gustily, Casey shook his head. "Not you, too."

"Sorry. It's a hazard of the job, I guess. I can't help but wonder about people who are so determined to keep secrets."

"Damn it, Andrew, people have a right to their secrets."

His smile crooked, Andrew murmured, "You remember what I do for a living, right?"

"Just how much has Natalie told you about why she left her firm in Nashville?" Aaron demanded.

"Nothing. And I didn't ask. Because it's none of my damned business," Casey answered almost savagely. "And whatever you found out, I don't want to—"

"She was fired, Case," Aaron said in a low, grim voice, as if he knew Casey wasn't going to like it but he had to say it, anyway. "Fired for selling confidential client information to the tabloid press."

"That's bull."

Andrew shook his head. "It's the truth. Her firm represented a lot of Nashville celebrities, several of whom were involved in various legal problems, and there were sleazy publications willing to pay for the details. The senior partners apparently thought there was enough evidence against Natalie to fire her. It was done discreetly, and Natalie didn't contest the action. She just left, and came here."

Casey was still shaking his head when Andrew finished speaking. "No. She wouldn't do anything like that."

"The facts were covered up by her firm because they didn't want the negative publicity," Aaron said. "They fired her without pursuing it any further because they wanted her and the potential scandal to disappear. Andrew found someone in the firm who was privy to the facts and was willing to share them with him."

For a price, Casey thought bitterly. Apparently, privacy ethics were rather loose in Natalie's former firm. But he could not accept that she would sell her own. "I don't believe it."

"There must have been some compelling evidence against her or she wouldn't have just gone quietly," Aaron argued. "She would have fought for her job."

Casey slammed a fist against the breakfast bar, making his cousins look at him in concern. "I don't want to hear any more of this. I am not gossiping about Natalie behind her back with you two."

"This isn't gossip, Case. This is fact," Andrew said evenly. "You might not like it, but that's what happened. We thought you should know."

"She's Jewel McDooley's niece, for God's sake. What on earth made you think you should run a background check on her?"

"Because we saw what Tamara did to you," Aaron said after a pause, completely serious for once. "You didn't believe the rumors about her, either, and when you were slapped in the face with the truth, it hurt you. We heard you were falling hard for another woman with big secrets, and we wanted to make sure you weren't hurt again."

He gave them both a hard look. "You overstepped your bounds," he said, his quiet tone seething with the emotions he wasn't able to suppress.

He snatched up his keys and wallet and headed for the door.

"Hey. Where are you going?"

"Out," he said without looking around in response to Aaron's question. "You guys can have dinner without me."

"Damn it, Case—"

But he'd already slammed the door behind him and was headed for his truck, having no interest in anything else his overly intrusive cousins had to say at that moment.

He climbed behind the wheel, started the engine and drove away from the cabin. And then pulled over to the side of the road and just sat there, staring blindly out the windshield. He didn't know where he was going.

The things Andrew and Aaron had told him about Natalie kept creeping into his mind, whispering doubts. He didn't want to believe any of it. And yet...

Why *had* she been so secretive? Wouldn't she have known he would believe her when she asserted her innocence?

If, of course, she was innocent.

He thought of the man he'd seen leaving her cabin before noon on Friday. She had to have known Casey had seen him, that he'd been curious, but she'd deliberately made no mention of the guy. Who was he? Was he somehow involved in this whole mess?

No. He shook his head with a scowl, thinking of the things he had gotten to know about Natalie during the past few days. She hadn't told him specifics about her life, her career, but he'd spent a lot of time with her. He'd gotten to know her pretty well.

Of course, he'd thought he knew Tamara well, too. And he had known her for several years before he'd found out how wrong he was about her. He'd spent only a couple of weeks with Natalie.

Yet, as Aaron had so accurately pointed out, he had fallen hard.

Aaron had also reminded him how badly Tamara had hurt

him, Casey thought, his fingers tightening around the steering wheel. Not because he had been so deeply in love with her, he knew now. But because he had trusted her. And that trust had been painfully abused.

The thought of being so bitterly disillusioned again...well, he had to admit it scared him a little. And that was an admission of vulnerability he didn't like making.

Natalie was surprised to hear a knock on her door at just after eight that evening. Recognizing the three rapid taps Casey always used to announce himself, she turned off the rather dull television program she'd been watching and moved across the room.

"Casey?" she asked, opening the door. "Is something wrong?"

Bending to pat Buddy, who'd ambled up to meet him, Casey said without looking at her, "I need to talk to you about something. I'm sorry if I'm disturbing you, but I couldn't wait until tomorrow."

That didn't sound encouraging. She glanced at the door he had closed behind himself. "Where are your cousins?"

He straightened, and for just a moment she saw what might have been a flash of irritation in his eyes. "They're back at my cabin, I guess. Or having dinner. I don't know."

"You've quarreled with them?"

"Yeah. But that's not why I'm here. Or, rather, it is—but... Damn it."

His uncharacteristically awkward stammering might have amused her had he not looked so grim. She motioned toward the couch. "Have a seat. Can I get you anything?"

"No. Thanks."

"Are you sure? If you haven't had dinner, I've got some..."

"I'm not hungry."

That sounded even more serious, since Casey had the typical

young man's hearty appetite. "What is this about?" she asked a bit nervously now.

Ignoring her invitation to sit, he paced to the fireplace, staring down at the dark grate. She hadn't bothered with a fire that evening, and the room felt suddenly cold and dark, as if he'd brought the chilly night in with him when he'd entered. Seeming to sense Casey's mood, Buddy sat on the hearth rug and gazed up at him, spine straight, his tail still.

Casey didn't seem to be in any hurry to start the conversation he said they needed. She perched on the edge of a chair, her fingers locked in front of her as she waited for him to answer her question.

When he finally spoke, his words caught her by surprise. "My family has had more than our share of drama through the years," he said, causing her to frown. That was hardly the way she had expected him to lead off.

"I suppose most families have," she offered tentatively.

"I told you about my dad and his siblings being separated and then finding each other again years later."

Even though he wasn't looking at her, she nodded.

He must have seen her from the corner of his eye, because he continued, "My aunt Michelle—the one who was adopted by the wealthy family and initiated the search for her siblings?"

"Yes, I remember you telling me about her. She married the private investigator."

"Right. Tony D'Alessandro. Anyway, Michelle was kidnapped when she was just a little girl and held for ransom for several days by a former family employee."

Shocked, she said, "What a terrifying ordeal that must have been for her. Was she hurt?"

"Not physically, no. But you can imagine that it was a horrifying event that haunted her for a long time."

She wasn't sure what this had to do with her, but she nodded somberly. "It must have."

"That wasn't the only traumatic event that members of my family have endured. My aunt Lindsey had a similar kidnapping experience several years later. My uncle Jared was once wrongly accused of robbery and was thrown in jail until he could prove his innocence. My parents met when my grandfather, a prosecuting attorney, hired my dad to protect my mother from some gang members who wanted to snatch my mom for leverage against Granddad in a big court trial."

Her head was spinning a little from all those dramatic details. "Your family *has* endured a lot," she conceded, her voice rising a bit in question.

"That history has left us—some of us, anyway—a little paranoid. And then there's the fact that several of my close relatives, including my dad and my cousin, Andrew, are private investigators and security consultants. Put a mystery in front of them and they seem compelled to dig into it. Especially if they think one of the family is in a position to be hurt by it."

She was growing more confused by the minute. "I don't—"

"Apparently, Aaron's been calling Molly during the past week, trying to find out how I've been doing and what was keeping me here so long," Casey cut in bluntly. "Molly's a sweetheart, but sometimes she talks too much. She mentioned that I've been seeing you, and I think she told him that I was pretty obviously infatuated by you."

Feeling her cheeks warm a little, Natalie looked back down at her hands. "So your cousins rushed out here to save you from me?"

Casey drew a deep breath and blurted, "Molly told them you lost your job with the law firm. I don't think she meant to let it slip, but Aaron's pretty good at weaseling information out of people, almost before they realize it. Anyway, Andrew did a little snooping, I guess, and…well, I'm very sorry, Natalie, but he told me what happened to you in Nashville."

Natalie felt her eyes go wide, the blood draining from her face. "He had no right to do that!"

Casey turned toward her then, holding up both hands, palms outward. "I know, and I told him the same thing. That's why I had to get away from them for a while. I was so mad I wasn't in the mood to deal with them."

She pushed herself out of her chair and began to pace in agitation. Buddy swiveled his head to watch her. This was so not the way she had wanted Casey to hear about what had happened to her, without even a chance for her to tell her side of the story. "Why would they investigate me, just because you and I have spent a few days together? What did they think I was going to do to you?"

He pushed his hand through his hair in a weary gesture. "It's hardly an excuse, but they've been worried about me. None of them really understood why I felt the need to take off when I did. It's the first time in my life I've ever been irresponsible, other than the pranks we played as kids. My mother thinks I'm on the verge of a breakdown, which is ridiculous. So…they heard I've been spending time with a woman who has a few secrets and they overreacted. I'm not defending them, I just know how they think."

Clutching her arms against a chill that was as much emotional as physical, she muttered, "When they found out what secret I've been keeping, they must have totally freaked out. I must really be out to con you, huh?"

Casey moved to stand in front of her, blocking her agitated pacing. "No one said anything about you trying to con me."

"They just think I had a very good reason for not telling you about what happened in Nashville, right? Like maybe I'm guilty of exactly what I was accused of doing."

"They didn't make any judgments about that," he said, though she noted he couldn't quite meet her eyes. "They simply told me the facts about what happened."

"Oh, really?" She planted her hands on her hips, glaring at him. "And just what 'facts' did they share with you?"

"I'm sure you know what they were told."

"I'd like to hear it from you," she insisted, wondering who in her former firm had been talking about her, and how those "facts" were being spun.

Looking extremely uncomfortable, Casey shoved his hands in his pockets. "They, um, heard that you sold confidential client information to the tabloids. Celebrity clients, sleazy gossip magazines. They said the senior partners found out about it and let you go quietly because they didn't want the negative publicity to reflect badly on the firm and cause other clients to lose faith in them. And that you left without fighting the charges."

"And what does *that* tell you?" she asked bitterly.

"That there must be a hell of a lot more to the story than my cousins found out," he replied evenly.

"So that's why you came running over here? To give me a chance to tell you my side?"

His eyes narrowed, as if her display of temper was triggering his own. "I came here because I thought you deserved to know what my cousins had done," he almost snapped. "Their invasion of your privacy was inexcusable, as I told them, myself."

"You're right. It was. I haven't even told my aunt what happened. Oh, God, you don't think your cousins..."

"They won't tell your aunt," he interrupted firmly. "They

haven't told Molly. Andrew and Aaron and I are the only ones here who know."

"That's bad enough," she grumbled, crossing her arms again and turning away. "Do you have any idea how humiliating this is for me?"

His tone gentled. "I can imagine."

Placing his hands on her shoulders, he turned her to face him again. "You don't owe me any explanations, Natalie. What happened to you is no more my business than it was my cousins'. But if you want to tell me, if you want my help...I'm here."

Still stinging because the choice to tell him was taken away from her, she asked, "What do you think? Do *you* believe I did what they said?"

"I'd like to hear your side."

"Spoken like a true lawyer," she said, pulling away from him and taking a few steps back. "You're keeping an open mind while you listen to the defendant's story, right? It's not *your* place to determine guilt or innocence."

"No, it's not." He sounded as if he were clinging to his patience with some difficulty. "But I didn't automatically believe what Andrew told me, either."

"How magnanimous of you."

"You aren't being exactly fair."

"It's a matter of trust," she whispered, turning her head to hide a sudden, mortifying rush of tears. "Do you trust me or not?"

The silence that fell between them then broke her heart. This, she thought dully, was exactly why she hadn't told Casey the truth from the start.

He couldn't see her face, because she had turned away from him. He could read her emotions in the slump of her shoulders, and he hated himself for what his instinctive hesitation had done to her.

Since he had met her, he'd seen Natalie defensive, guarded, amused, relaxed, even cautiously flirtatious. He'd watched her open herself to Buddy—and to him, in some ways. But he had never seen her looking defeated. Until now.

"I've had some trouble with trusting lately," he said, his voice sounding a bit loud in the too-quiet room. "A couple of people I trusted let me down. Hard. I guess you could say that's why I'm here, pretending to be a handyman. I needed to think some things through, put them into perspective."

"I hope you've had more luck with that than I have," she murmured, still looking away.

"I thought I had," he replied. "I thought I'd gotten over it completely. Apparently, I was wrong."

"I don't know what you mean."

Moving to stand behind her, he rested his hands on her shoulders, which went rigid beneath his touch. "I didn't realize it until now, but I let my recent disillusionment color my reactions to what my cousins told me about you. I didn't immediately jump to your defense because I didn't want to have my trust betrayed again if I found out I was wrong about you. It was a stupid, cowardly response on my part. I'm sorry."

"You're saying you suddenly believe I'm innocent?" she asked, understandably skeptical.

"I'm saying that if I've learned anything about you during the last couple of weeks, it's that you are honest. Almost to a fault, sometimes," he added with a wry smile. "You asked if I trust you. I'm sorry it took me so long to answer. Yes, Natalie. I trust you. I don't believe you sold your ethics for cash."

"You can't know that," she countered, her head still lowered.

"I haven't told you anything about myself. Even when you told me you're an attorney, I didn't tell you I am, too."

"No. I can understand now why you didn't."

"It was too humiliating."

"I know. I suppose I should confess that I was already aware of your profession when I told you what I do. All I knew was that you were a lawyer, and that you were between jobs."

She looked over her shoulder at him. "How did you know?"

His mouth crooked. "Molly let it slip to me, too."

"I don't think I'd ever share a big secret with your cousin Molly," she resolved with a little shake of her head.

He chuckled. "I know it sounds that way, but Molly has been known to keep secrets. Anyway, I only found out your profession a couple of days ago. That's why I thought I should tell you what I do, and then let you fill me in on whatever you wanted me to know in your own time. I swear to you, I made no effort to find out anything about you that you didn't tell me yourself. I didn't ask Andrew and Aaron to snoop. I would have ordered them not to if they'd bothered to tell me what they were doing."

"I guess it doesn't really matter now," she muttered, sounding suddenly weary. "Everyone will probably find out eventually. Especially when I can't find another job because no one will want to hire an attorney who's been accused of selling confidential client information."

He moved to stand in front of her, looking down at her dejected expression. He still felt like a heel for being partially responsible for the sadness in her eyes. "You didn't do it," he said, and it wasn't a question.

"No. But that doesn't matter. I've done everything I know how to do to prove that someone set me up to take the blame for those leaks. I have a few leads, but no solid evidence. And without incontrovertible evidence, it's my word against the firm's. No one will believe me."

"I just mentioned that several of my relatives are P.I.s. Despite my present irritation with him, I know Andrew's very good at his job. Tell him the details, give him the names of anyone you suspect, and let him see what he can find out. Let us help you clear your name."

She shook her head. "I already have a P.I. His name is Rand Beecham. You saw him leaving yesterday morning."

A P.I. He didn't want to admit how much it had bothered him to see a man leaving her cabin, how hard it had been for him not to ask who he was—or how very relieved he was to hear her explanation. This wasn't the time to go into his feelings. For now, they needed to concentrate on facts.

"He's a P.I.? From Nashville?"

She nodded. "An ex-cop. I, um, found him in the yellow pages."

She looked both embarrassed and frustrated by that admission, as if she were less than pleased with her employee. "Has he found anything to prove your innocence?"

She twisted her fingers in front of her, looking down at her hands. "He's pursuing a couple of leads."

Watching her closely, he prodded, "You're satisfied that he's good at what he does?"

"I—" She spread her hands. "I don't know what else to do," she admitted. "I've tried doing some research on my own, but I've got to admit I don't have the faintest idea where to start. I've typed dozens of names into search engines, but I haven't found anything to indicate anyone I know would do this to me."

"Would you mind if Andrew does some investigating on the side? Maybe a pair of fresh eyes will find something you and Beecham have missed."

"I, um—" She bit her lip, not knowing quite how to say that she could barely afford one P.I., much less two.

"Andrew wouldn't charge for his time, of course," Casey added. "We don't charge friends. Besides, he owes you this. Like you said, he had no right to invade your privacy. The least he can do is help clear your name."

"I can't ask him to do that."

"You don't have to. I'll ask him."

She drew an unsteady breath. "You haven't heard the whole story. The evidence against me—"

"I don't care," he said evenly. "You didn't do it."

"There are plenty of people who believe I did. People who've known me a lot longer than you have."

He shrugged. "Some of them are idiots. Others may not necessarily disbelieve you, they just don't want to get involved."

"That's exactly what I got from a lot of them. As if my bad luck would rub off on them if they stayed too close to me."

He reached out to cover her hand with his. "I'm sorry. You must have been feeling very alone."

"Not so much lately," she admitted, and he was pleased that she left her hand in his. "Thank you for that."

"It was, quite literally, my pleasure."

She released a long, pent-up breath. As much as she still obviously hated the way he'd found out, he wondered if she felt some relief in having him know the truth about what had happened to her.

"Let us help you, Natalie."

"You don't even know if your cousin would be willing to help," she pointed out a little shakily.

"He'll help."

For the first time since he had arrived that evening, she smiled, though weakly. "Why do I have a sudden mental image of you putting your P.I. cousin in a headlock until he agrees to help me?"

"If that's what it takes," he said lightly, grateful that her tension was easing, if only a little. "I'll bring the twins over first thing in the morning. You can tell Andrew everything that happened, everything you've found out since you left the firm, and we'll see what he has to say. If he has any questions, he can tap the resources of our fathers' firm. We'll figure out what's going on, Natalie, and we'll prove that you had nothing to do with those leaks."

She looked up at him searchingly. "Why would you do this?"

He smiled. "You really have to ask?"

Lowering his head, he gave her a long, achingly tender kiss. She was clinging to his shirt by the time the kiss ended.

As much as he wanted to keep kissing her, he knew this was the wrong time. She was too vulnerable tonight. For that matter, he was, himself, a bit. They both needed some time to regroup. He made himself draw back, and she didn't try to detain him.

"You'll let us help you?" he asked.

She swallowed and nodded. "I'm willing to try, if your cousin is agreeable. And if Beecham doesn't come through first."

He allowed himself one slow stroke of her cheek. "Get some sleep tonight, Natalie. We're going to take care of this."

"You're leaving now?"

He nodded. "I've gotta go yell at my cousins some more for invading your privacy. And then I'll tell them that to make up for it, they're going to help you."

"Don't you want to ask me any more questions about what happened?"

"I'll wait until you tell Andrew in the morning. There's no need for you to have to go through it all twice."

She drew a deep breath and nodded. "All right. I'll tell Andrew everything I know."

"Sounds good. See you in the morning." He looked at her for a moment longer, then moved toward the door.

"Casey?"

Already halfway outside, he looked around to see her standing beside the couch, Buddy at her side as they watched him walk away. "Yes?"

"Thank you for believing in me."

He smiled and stepped outside, closing the door behind him.

Chapter Twelve

"I don't appreciate the way you invaded my privacy without my permission and without any justification. You went completely over the line with that."

Andrew Walker accepted Natalie's criticism without flinching, his expression impossible for her read. "I apologize," he said quietly. "It's a habit I've gotten into in my job—researching people, I mean. I didn't hack into any of your personal accounts or anything, if you're worried about that. Most of what I found was common knowledge among your coworkers in the firm."

"Most." She seized on that word. "The firm didn't publicize why they let me go. That was kept secret—more for the sake of their own reputation than out of any respect for me," she added resentfully. "You wouldn't have found that just by typing my name into a search engine."

"I made a couple of calls," he admitted. "The very secrecy

of your firing piqued my curiosity. You'd apparently been doing very well at the firm, steadily climbing the ladder, earning a name for yourself, keeping a high profile in the profession— and then suddenly you were gone and no one was talking. That usually indicates a cover-up of some sort."

"Who did you call?"

"Just a couple of sources in your area," he replied vaguely.

Which meant he wasn't going to tell her.

Having stood back with Casey while Natalie raked his brother over the coals, Aaron stepped forward then. "It wasn't entirely Andrew's fault. I sort of nagged him into looking into your background. I mean, I could tell that Molly and Kyle like you and I know they think the world of your aunt and uncle, but Molly seemed to think there was something going on with you.

"Not that she said anything specifically," he added quickly, loyally defending his cousin. "She was just very vague about why you were here, probably because she didn't know, herself. With all the problems Casey's been through lately, I was concerned about him getting mixed up in someone else's troubles and risking his own reputation back in Dallas."

"Sticking your nose into my business," Casey muttered.

Aaron sighed deeply. "We had this talk last night," he reminded Casey. "Extensively. I've apologized to you, and now I'm trying to apologize to Natalie."

"You aren't apologizing, you're rationalizing."

Natalie lifted a hand to ward off what sounded like an impending argument. "Okay, the thing is, I didn't appreciate the snooping. But I am grateful for the offer of assistance, if you really think you can help."

"I can help," Andrew said. "But first, I think I should tell you what I've found out about Rand Beecham."

She frowned at him. "Rand Beecham?"

He nodded. "When Casey told me last night that you'd hired Beecham and haven't been entirely satisfied with his work, I made some calls."

It was all she could do not to pull her own hair. "You mean you've made calls about me without my permission again? Even after Casey told you how upset I was with you the first time?"

Looking a bit surprised that she'd have any problem with what he had done, Andrew nodded. "Casey said you wanted our help. The first step was obviously to find out more about the guy who's been working for you."

She shook her head. "Has anyone ever mentioned that you have personal boundary issues?"

Both Aaron and Casey smirked as if they'd heard that accusation leveled toward Andrew before. Andrew, himself, merely shrugged. "I just think you should know that you can't necessarily trust everything Beecham says. He's been in some trouble before."

"That doesn't surprise me," she said. "But I've insisted on an accounting of the work he does for me. I didn't intend to pay him without challenging some of the charges, which I could tell were somewhat inflated. And I told him I expected results within the next few days or I was terminating our professional relationship."

Andrew nodded. "I wouldn't hold my breath for those results, though you can probably expect another request for more money. Apparently, that's how he operates. He dribbles out a little information while billing the clients for as long as they'll let him."

Because Andrew was making her feel a bit foolish, she spoke curtly. "I'd already pretty much figured that out. I just told you, I wasn't going to let him get away with it much longer."

"I'm not going to worry about stepping on Beecham's professional toes while I find out what I can about your situation."

She cocked her head to study him curiously. "Do you ever worry about stepping on toes?"

Andrew gave her a quick smile. "Not a lot, no. And speaking of which—you said you had nothing to do with the tabloid leaks?"

"That's right," she said firmly. "I had *nothing* to do with them. I would never violate confidentiality, not for my own clients and not for any of the firm's other clients."

"Then we'll find out what happened," Andrew asserted with a confidence that was strangely reassuring. "I just need to know the details."

"Let's all sit down and get comfortable for this," Casey said, motioning toward the couch and chairs.

"I'll put on a fresh pot of coffee," Natalie said, turning toward the kitchen. She needed just a few more minutes to prepare herself for what was coming.

"Is there anything I can do to help?" Casey asked.

"No, I've got it. You might see if Buddy needs to go out before we start."

"He's a nice dog," Aaron said, watching as Casey opened the door for Buddy to go out. "Have you had him long?"

"Actually, he's a stray," Natalie replied. "He showed up here a few days ago and Casey and I sort of took him in. I have inquiries out to find his previous owners, but so far no one's called."

"Hey, maybe Andy needs to investigate the dog, too," Aaron quipped. When no one laughed, he sighed and sank into a chair.

A few minutes later they were all sitting around the living room with cups of coffee. Natalie held hers because it gave her something to do with her hands, but she barely tasted the hot beverage.

Taking a deep breath, she haltingly told the story of how she'd been fired from her position in Nashville. She confessed that she'd been a workaholic who'd spent nearly every waking moment either at the office or working at home. That she'd seen her efforts pay off when she began to move up in the firm, sometimes ahead of other associates who'd been there longer.

"I didn't deliberately climb over anyone on my way up," she added quickly, "and I tried not to make any enemies during the process. But in a fiercely cutthroat and ruthlessly profitable firm like Bennings, Heaton, Schroeder and Merkel, there are always going to be those who resent any accomplishments made by the people the associates regard as competitors."

"Did you know about the tabloid leaks?" Andrew asked.

She shrugged. "Everyone knew that certain things were showing up in the press that shouldn't be public knowledge. Everyone was beginning to whisper, wondering if anyone we knew was behind the indiscretions. Some people claimed the leaks couldn't possibly have come from inside the firm, that the tidbits were being released by outside sources with connections to the clients, themselves. That was what I wanted to believe."

And then one day three weeks ago, she continued, she had been called into a senior partner's office and summarily dismissed for "flagrant indiscretions." Despite her stunned protestations of innocence, she'd been presented with evidence of her guilt. She was fired with the warning that if she said anything about the firm or her reason for leaving, information that would be very embarrassing to the company that prided itself on the privacy it offered its wealthy and high-profile clients, they would aggressively pursue having her publicly disbarred.

She had tried to tell the story without emotion, keeping her voice steady, her expression blank, but apparently she hadn't hidden her tumultuous feelings from Casey. Sitting beside her on the couch, he reached out to lay a hand on her thigh, just above her knee, his fingers squeezing lightly, supportively.

"What was the evidence you were shown?" Andrew asked, already making notes in a pad he'd brought with him.

"Several photocopies of checks made out in my name from a tabloid reporter. The checks were dated around the same times that the leaks occurred. Needless to say, I never received those checks. Someone had to forge my name to cash them."

"Where did the senior partner get those photocopies?"

"He said they were provided by an anonymous source. Someone who had stumbled onto the truth and thought it should be brought to light. To me, that ridiculous explanation made it obvious that someone was setting me up to take the blame for the leaks, but Herb just brushed off everything I said. He refused to believe I'd been framed. He called that the oldest excuse in the book."

"The photocopies of the checks were all the evidence he had?"

"No. There were also copies of e-mails sent from my computer at the firm to that same sleazy reporter. I didn't send them, but they had my e-mail address on them."

"Wouldn't you have noticed if you'd gotten any return e-mail from the reporter?" Aaron asked.

"The e-mails I was shown instructed the guy not to reply to that address. Instead, they said he was to make contact 'through the usual means,' whatever that entailed."

"Did you try to contact that reporter to make him admit he hadn't been talking to you?" Casey asked.

"He wouldn't take my calls. Nor would he talk to me when I tried to show up at his door. He said if I continued to try to contact him, he would inform the firm that I was causing trouble."

"You've had more than your share of threats lately," Casey muttered, and he sounded angry on her behalf.

She nodded. "That was all the so-called evidence my superiors had on me, but it was enough for them to believe I was guilty. And it was an easy solution for them. Get rid of me, sweep any potential scandal under the rug, go on with business as usual."

"Have you been in touch with any of your former associates?"

She shook her head in response to Andrew's question. "They act as though I'm in quarantine. If it hadn't been for Amber, I wouldn't know what was going on there."

"Amber?"

"Amber Keller, my former clerical assistant. She's still there, working for another attorney, Stephen Gilbert, but she calls me every few days to let me know if she's heard anything. Amber stuck by me. She's the only one who has believed me from the start."

"As your assistant, Amber would have had access to your accounts, wouldn't she? Maybe even your social security number?"

Natalie set her coffee cup down with a thump, frowning at Andrew. "Weren't you listening to me? I said Amber was on my side. From the beginning."

Andrew glanced up at her, and the expression in his dark eyes looked entirely too cynical for a man five years her junior. "Sometimes the people we trust most are the ones who do the most harm," he said flatly. "If it turns out that she's involved, she wouldn't be the first to claim loyalty to deflect the blame from herself."

Both Aaron and Casey were looking somberly at Andrew, as if they knew he spoke from experience when it came to betrayal, but Natalie shook her head. "That doesn't even make sense. Why would she be calling me to give me updates if she'd had anything to do with it?"

"Maybe to see if you've made any progress in your research," Aaron suggested. "You know that old advice about keeping your friends close and your enemies closer."

"I am not Amber's enemy. Nor is she mine. She's a friend. One of the few I have left after this debacle."

"Sounds to me like you didn't have very good friends," Aaron muttered.

Natalie bit her lip, thinking she'd come to that same realization recently. Casey squeezed her knee again.

"You should check out Cathy Linski," she told Andrew, and spelled the name for him.

He wrote it down, making notes about what Amber had said about Cathy's recent windfall and about what Beecham had told her. "I'll look into it," he said. "Anyone else?"

She shrugged with the feeling of helplessness that had overwhelmed her every time she'd tried to narrow down a list of suspects. "There are so many people at the firm. I just don't know."

"What about men? Were you romantically involved with anyone at the firm?"

Casey shifted on the couch, muttering, "Andrew."

His cousin merely glanced at him. He hadn't minced words about Natalie's friend, and he wouldn't about this, either, his expression implied.

"There's a guy I went out with for a short time, though it wasn't really all that serious," she admitted reluctantly. "We dated for about three months. His name is Thad Wolff, but I doubt that he had anything to do with this. He hasn't been with the firm all that long and he's definitely looking to move up. He dumped me like a toxic chemical as soon as there was the faintest hint that I was in trouble."

"No one else?"

"No. I haven't really had time to date much in the past couple of years. All I've focused on was my job."

And now that was gone, she thought glumly. Leaving her with…what? A ruined reputation, no friends, dwindling savings, and a foolish heart that was about to be battered again when her reckless vacation flirtation with Casey ended, as it soon would.

"Is there anything else you can think of to tell me?" Andrew asked, studying her a bit too closely.

"That's all."

"Would you mind giving me your cell number in case I come up with any more questions?"

She recited the number to him and watched him jot it down in his precise, neat handwriting. "What will you do now?"

Folding the notebook, he slipped it into the pocket of the blue cotton shirt he wore with his jeans. "I'm going to Nashville."

"Oh. If the senior partners find out I have a private investigator looking into this—much less two…"

He flicked her a look that made her fall silent. "They won't find out until you're ready for them to," he said. "I'll talk to Beecham first, find out if there's anything he hasn't told you. You'll probably be getting a call from him, asking if you really sent me. He'll probably try to nag you into calling me off and letting him keep billing you."

"I'll call Beecham."

"No. Wait until he calls you. I don't want him to have advance notice that I'm coming—just in case he decides to go to one of the suspects on your list and offer any evidence he has uncovered, for a nice price."

"You don't trust anyone, do you?"

Andrew shrugged. "I trust my family. Outside of that…only a select few."

"I see."

"Give me a few days and you'll be able to go back to your firm with a few threats of your own."

She wished she could be as certain about that as he seemed to be. She looked at Aaron. "Are you going to Nashville with him?"

Aaron shook his head. "I'm going back to Dallas to reassure my family that Casey hasn't gone off the deep end and that he'll be back as soon as he's finished helping Kyle and Molly here, probably next week."

It sounded like a rehearsed speech, one that Casey had likely drilled into him.

"Even though I would like to spend a little more time in this area," Aaron added a bit wistfully. "I love hiking and kayaking and mountain biking."

"You can come back and do all of that some other time," Casey assured him firmly. "You know Molly and Kyle always welcome visits from family."

Aaron sighed and nodded, conceding that he was being sent away.

The twins stayed long enough to admire the renovations outside the cabin, and to play a little ball with Buddy, who loved the attention. By the time they said their goodbyes, he was treating them like old friends.

As for Natalie, she couldn't say she had entirely forgiven them for invading her privacy before they'd even met her, but she could certainly appreciate their efforts on her behalf now. If Andrew really was able to clear her name, she supposed it would all be worth it.

"I'm sure Andrew will be able to help you," Aaron told her as he took his leave.

"Thank you. I hope so."

"He will," Aaron said assuredly. "And maybe I'll have the pleasure of seeing you again sometime."

"Maybe," she murmured, though she found it doubtful.

"I'll be in touch," Andrew told her, patting the pocket where he'd stashed his notebook.

She nodded. "If you find anything…"

"I'll call you," he promised.

The twins said their goodbyes to Casey, and she could see the strongly fraternal affection among the three, despite Casey's leftover annoyance at his cousins' behavior. He'd get over it soon enough, especially if Andrew came through with the answer to Natalie's problems.

Casey wouldn't let her come between him and his family, she mused, watching the twins stride away. She couldn't imagine he would allow anyone to do that, much less someone who was only temporarily in his life.

Casey slipped his arms around her waist from behind. "So," he murmured into her ear, "about this Thad jerk."

She couldn't help smiling, as he had undoubtedly intended. "What about him?"

"Was he better-looking than me?"

She turned in his arms, resting her hands on his chest. "No way."

"We'll forget about him then."

"I already have," she assured him with a smile.

He kissed her lightly, then raised his head. "Do you want me to leave, too?"

She didn't even hesitate. "No."

"Want to go for a walk?"

"Yes, I'd like that."

Taking her hand, he led her toward the creek that ran alongside the back of the property, into the patchy woods that surrounded the cabin. It was a cloudy day, and chilly, but her jacket, sweater and jeans kept her reasonably warm. Casey's proximity raised her body temperature another couple of degrees as he walked so close that their shoulders brushed.

Buddy accompanied them, occasionally dashing off to sniff the ground or scratch in the leaves. She wondered if he was revisiting places he'd been while he'd lived out here alone in the woods. She couldn't get over how much healthier and more carefree he looked since the first time she had seen him.

"I am so sorry about what you've been through," Casey said after a while, his tone grave. "This whole thing must have felt like a nightmare to you."

"Yes, pretty much. I kept telling Herb that I had nothing to do with the leaks, but he just wouldn't listen."

"Does anyone in your family know what happened?"

"I told my mother that I had a falling out with a senior partner and left the firm. That upset her, but not as much as the whole truth would have. I told Aunt Jewel pretty much the same story, for the same reason. It wasn't a lie. It just wasn't the whole truth."

"You didn't want them to worry."

"No. My dad knows more of the details. He wanted to charge home and help me get a lawyer of my own and 'sue the bastards into bankruptcy,' as he put it, but I knew I'd have to have more evidence to back up my story if I was going to even try to fight the accusations. That's why I hired Beecham, though it's obvious I had no idea how to hire a private investigator. He convinced me that he knew what he was doing and that he would be very discreet, but I just don't think he's very good."

"Andrew is."

"That's what you and Aaron keep telling me."

"Trust us."

She bent down to pick up an interesting pebble beside the creek. A very pale gray, it was shaped roughly like a heart with a small crack in the center. Though she found that symbolism a little too ironic, she slipped it in her jacket pocket, anyway.

"Will you go back to the firm?" Casey asked. "After you prove your innocence, I mean?"

"I don't know. I haven't thought that far ahead."

He tossed a twig into the rushing water of the creek to watch it tumble down the rocks. Studying his expression, she asked, "Casey? Why is your family so worried about you?"

"You heard Aaron. They think I'm having a nervous breakdown."

"Because you took a vacation?"

He released a long, low breath. "I've had some… setbacks lately. Nothing like what you've been through."

"Those people who betrayed your trust?"

"Yeah." He put his free hand to the back of his neck and squeezed the muscles there as if they'd suddenly tightened. "It started when I lost a big case."

Raising an eyebrow, she murmured, "That happens to the best of us."

"But this was a particularly bad loss. I missed something in my preparation for the trial. Something pretty damned important."

"So you made a mistake. I hate to tell you, my friend, but it won't be the last one you make."

"It wasn't just that." Speaking in a low voice as they continued their stroll, he told her about the spoiled rich kid he'd gotten acquitted on a technicality for a vehicular manslaughter charge. The kid had promised everyone, including Casey, that he had learned his lesson and would never get behind the wheel of a car again after drinking.

Less than a year later, only weeks after Casey had lost the other big case, that self-absorbed and obscenely indulged teenager had driven drunk again and wrecked the third sports car his father had bought for him. A child in another car had been killed in the crash.

Her hand tightened spasmodically around his as she heard the pain in his voice. "Oh, Casey, surely you don't blame yourself for that. You did your job, nothing more. If anyone is to blame besides the boy, it's his parents."

"I know. I don't blame myself, exactly. I believe in what we do, and that we have to do our best for the people we represent no matter what our personal biases might be."

He seemed to be presenting an argument he'd made many times to people who were derogatory toward attorneys. She'd made much the same speech herself a few times. "But—"

"But," he said with a sigh, "sometimes I can't help but focus on the downside of that practice. Especially when I know it was money and connections as much as my skill that were responsible for putting my client back behind the wheel. A kid from a different part of town would have been assigned an overworked and underpaid public defender and he'd have been put behind bars."

"That's part of the reality of the job, too," Natalie murmured. "The best defense that money can buy."

He grimaced and nodded. "It just really shook me when I heard what happened right after the loss that should have been a win."

"So you took some time to rethink your career choice?"

"To rethink my options within the career, maybe," he said with a slight shrug.

"Have you reached any conclusions?"

"Not really. I'll probably just go back to what I was doing. I guess I just really needed a vacation."

"Not so much of a vacation. You've been working pretty hard around here."

He smiled. "I enjoyed working with my hands for a change. Made me feel…I don't know, more grounded or something."

"That makes sense. I enjoyed the days I spent helping you." She didn't know if that was due more to the work or to spending that time with Casey, but she suspected she knew the answer to that one.

"It wasn't just work I needed to get away from for a while,"

Casey said after a pause that suddenly seemed significant. "I was sort of engaged until a little over a month ago. The ending was harsh, and pretty tough on my ego, to be frank. She dumped me for a partner in a rival law firm. Now she's wearing a big rock on her hand and making sure everyone in the greater Texas social scene knows about it."

"You were…engaged?" Natalie repeated, feeling her stomach tighten.

"I said 'sort of' engaged," he corrected. "You know that stage where you talk about getting married someday and everyone pretty much expects it but it's not really official?"

She had never actually been in "that stage" herself, but she nodded. "I'm sorry."

He shook his head almost impatiently. "It's not like that. Things hadn't been that great between Tamara and me for quite a while. You know what it's like when you work all the time. Whole days would go by when I wouldn't even see her. The breakup was as much my fault as it was hers, it just caught me off guard. She could have handled it a little more discreetly, but I'm not sad that it's over."

"So, you lost a case, lost a 'sort of' fiancée and suffered a crisis of conscience all within a few months?"

"That about sums it up."

"No wonder you needed a vacation."

"Thank you."

Turning to lean against a crooked tree trunk, she studied his face as he threw a stick for Buddy. "Casey?"

"Mmm? Come on, Buddy, bring it back. Give it back to me. Fetch."

Buddy didn't seem to be getting the message. He picked up the stick and ran the other way with it.

Natalie smiled, but continued her line of thought. "Why

were you so secretive about what you do? I mean, I didn't want to explain why I'd been fired because…well, you understand. But you still have a position with your firm. You don't have anything to hide."

He straightened, turning to look at her with a wry smile. "At first it was because I was tired of explaining myself. Tired of answering questions about why I'd taken time off from a prestigious position to do maintenance work here. It was nice just to be a handyman with no expectations to live up to, you know?"

"That makes sense."

"And there was the fact that you never really asked me what I do," he added. "You didn't ask any questions about me at all. I wasn't sure you were interested."

"I didn't want to ask questions because I was afraid it would encourage you to do the same," she confessed.

"Yeah, I figured that out." He reached out to touch her cheek. "Your face is pink. Are you getting cold?"

"Maybe a little."

"Ready to go back to the cabin?"

"I suppose so."

He took her hand and whistled for Buddy, who was barking at a squirrel. "C'mon, Buddy. Let's go home."

Home. She thought about the word as they fell in step. The cabin wasn't home, she reminded herself. Not for any of the three of them. No matter how cozy it had become for them.

Chapter Thirteen

They worked on the grounds together for most of the afternoon, raking leaves, picking up sticks, pruning the evergreen bushes around the cabin, piling mulch around the other plants to protect them from the rapidly coming winter. In some ways, she and Casey were even more comfortable together now that their secrets were out in the open. Yet in other ways, there was a growing tension between them, and she knew what was causing that, too.

Every time their eyes met, her skin flushed and her pulse raced. Each time they touched, whether accidentally or on purpose, she felt electricity zing through her body, sparking heat deep inside her. Each stolen kiss lasted longer than the one before, and every embrace was greedier. Hungrier.

Though it was a cool day, they were both overheated by the time they'd finished their work and afternoon faded into early darkness. Sending Casey to the small front bath to wash up,

Natalie took a quick shower and changed into a clean sweater and jeans. When she rejoined him in the living room, she noted that his hair was wet and his skin scrubbed clean, though of course he wore the same slightly grubby clothes he'd had on before. They had a simple dinner of sandwiches and canned soup, lingering over the meal as if they were dining on fine cuisine.

Afterward, Natalie wandered to the glass door to look outside at the beautiful evening. It was too dark now to appreciate the view, but there was enough moonlight to frost with magic what she could see. Stars twinkled in the endless rural sky, undimmed by the bright city lights she was accustomed to seeing back home. She sighed lightly.

Casey's arms slipped around her from behind, and she leaned back into him. "It's a nice night, hmm?" he murmured in her ear, his breath warm against her skin.

"It's beautiful," she whispered, crossing her hands over his at her waist.

"You know what would feel really good right now?"

There were so many possible responses to that question. "Um—what?"

"That new hot tub. Maybe a glass of wine to sip while we enjoy the bubbles."

She could almost feel her knees weaken with the images he invoked, and she was grateful that he was supporting her. "That does sound nice."

"I'm sure Kyle would want us to make sure it's working correctly," he said, keeping his tone serious though there was a smile in his voice—as well as a question.

She turned her head to look at him, silently giving him her answer, though she played along. "I'm not sure why you think it would take both of us to test it."

He shook his head, tsking his tongue in disapproval. "Don't

you know you're never supposed to go into the water alone? You could drown."

"I think that rule applies to swimming, not soaking."

He ran a hand up her arm, even as he bent his head to press a kiss against the back of her neck. "Really? 'Cause I think I heard it applies to hot tubs, as well."

Her eyelids grew heavy as he nibbled and licked the sensitive skin at her nape. Pressed snugly against Casey's full length, she felt the evidence of how badly he wanted her, how difficult it must be for him to keep his tone teasing.

Turning in his arms, she pressed lightly against him and walked the fingers of her right hand up his chest. "But I didn't pack a bathing suit. And I know you don't have one with you."

She was rewarded for her own teasing by a dark flush of color on his cheeks, a glint of passion in his eyes. "I suppose we'll just have to—" he paused to clear his husky voice "—improvise."

Running her fingertips along his jawline, she murmured, "I'll get some towels."

She saw him swallow before he nodded. "I'll pour the wine."

Standing in the bedroom, she pushed a hand through her hair as she drew a deep breath to steady herself. Yet her hands still trembled a bit as she stripped off her clothes and wrapped herself in her favorite, red silk kimono.

The living room was empty when she returned with two big, fluffy towels. Stepping outside, she found Casey already in the tub. He looked relaxed and comfortable as he lounged in the molded seat, his neck supported by a cushioned headrest. He'd turned off the bright deck lights, so that the only illumination came from the soft blue LED lights within the tub itself. Only partially concealed by the swirling, foaming bubbles, his body was a lean, tan outline beneath the water.

Only then did she notice the stack of clothing neatly folded on the bench built into the deck railing. The expression in his eyes hidden in the shadows, he nodded to the space beside him and the extra glass of wine sitting on the built-in tray beside it. "This feels as good as I thought it would. Come on in. I saved a place for you."

Without looking away from his face, she dropped the towels onto the bench beside his clothes, then untied her kimono. The garment slithered to her feet. And suddenly Casey didn't look nearly as relaxed.

The hot water swirled around her ankle, her calf as she stepped into the tub. Very slowly, she submerged herself to her shoulders, sighing as the hidden jets gently pulsed against her weary muscles. "Oh, that does feel good," she murmured, letting her head fall back against the cushioned rest.

Stretching out very close to her, Casey reached over to take her hand beneath the water. She turned her head to smile at him. Taking their time and testing their patience, they lay there for several long, quiet minutes, their fingers laced, their wine-glasses held in their free hands as they sipped and gazed out at the clear, jeweled night sky. The mountains ahead of them were dark shapes against the slightly lighter sky, and a choir of night creatures softly serenaded them.

"This is amazing," she said on a sigh. "Wouldn't it be lovely to sit out here and watch the snow fall?"

"Yeah. That would be cool. Er, no pun intended."

She smiled. "I've got to admit, this spa was a good idea."

"A very good idea," he murmured, leaning over to taste her bare shoulder. "Did I ever mention you look really good wet? I've thought so since the day I sprayed you down in your kitchen."

"You really shouldn't remind me of that. I thought you were the worst handyman I'd ever met. And the sexiest," she added with a low laugh.

"Really?" His lips had moved to her throat.

Tipping her head back, she closed her eyes. "Mmm-hmm."

"What do you think of me now?" he asked, taking the wine-glass from her hand and setting it aside.

She wrapped her arms around him. "I think you're a bit better handyman than I originally believed. But still the sexiest."

He smiled against her lips. "Thank you."

Pulling him closer, she murmured, "You're welcome."

He slipped his wet fingers into her hair, bringing her face to his, nibbling a kiss against her lips. Beneath the water, she stroked her smooth calf against his hair-roughened one, loving the contrast.

The kisses deepened, tongues exploring, tangling. He slid his hand to her breasts, cupping one at a time, his thumb making lazy circles until she was arching eagerly into him, groping for him. When she found him, hard and ready, he drew in a deep, sharp breath and shifted until she was partially beneath him, their bodies moving slickly, hungrily.

From that first time she had seen him in his jeans and tool belt, his lazy smile lighting his fallen-angel face, she had wanted him. That desire had only grown as she'd gotten to know him better, watching him charm babies and stray animals, seeing the way he'd quietly fought his own inner battles, the way he was so willing to help fight hers.

Casey Walker was a very special man, and she could think of no other way to tell him how much she admired him. How much she genuinely liked him. If there was more to it than that…well, she would deal with that later. Tonight was to relish, a perfect gem of a memory to be tucked away against whatever might happen between them later.

His hand slid up her thigh to brush against her core and she gasped into his mouth. Moments later she nearly whimpered when he began to stroke and gently probe. She tried to draw him closer, but he resisted, his mouth at her breasts now, his fingers skillfully playing her until there wasn't a rational thought left in her mind. She climaxed with a strangled cry, her body arching almost out of the water.

Casey surged upward, carrying her with him as he climbed out of the tub. They toweled off hastily, just enough that they wouldn't drip all over the cabin floors and then Casey snatched up his clothes and they moved inside. Buddy was curled into his usual spot on the hearth rug, giving them complete privacy as they headed for the bedroom, closing the door behind them.

Casey fumbled in the pocket of his jeans, then threw them recklessly aside to take her in his arms again. His mouth covered hers even before her back hit the mattress. His patience was obviously completely gone now, but he managed to slow down long enough to bring her to a new peak of pleasure again before he sought his own release.

Buried deeply inside her, he shuddered and murmured her name against her lips, the broken tenderness of his tone bringing tears to her eyes. She blinked them back and held him fiercely, willing the clock to slow down so she could savor every moment of this night with him.

Natalie's cell phone rang Monday morning, startling her awake. After a night of very little sleep, she and Casey had slept in. She gave herself just a moment to look at him blinking himself awake on the pillow next to her before pushing herself upright and snatching the phone off the nightstand.

She checked the caller ID. "It's Beecham," she said and lifted the phone to her ear. "Hello."

"Who the hell is this Walker guy?" Beecham demanded angrily. "He visited me this morning, said he's from some big, hotshot investigation and security firm in Dallas and that he's taking over your case."

"Yes, Andrew Walker is working for me," she replied smoothly. "Send me your final bill, Mr. Beecham, and I'll call you to settle on a final accounting of what, if anything, I owe you."

"You're firing me?"

"I'm terminating our professional relationship," she answered evenly. "I'll expect you to maintain our confidentiality agreement, of course."

Beecham argued with her a bit longer, but she remained steadfast that his services were no longer needed. He was still sputtering when she disconnected the call.

"You handled that very smoothly," Casey said, kissing the back of her bare shoulder. "You didn't sound like someone I'd want to argue with."

"I hope you're right about how good your cousin is at his job," she replied a bit shakily. "By firing Beecham, I've put my future career in Andrew's hands."

"You won't be sorry."

"I hope you're right," she repeated, and then tried to push her fears aside, since worrying about it wasn't accomplishing anything.

After a late, leisurely breakfast, she and Casey stopped by his cabin for him to change clothes and then went for a drive through Cades Cove, a lush valley tucked into the mountains not far from Gatlinburg. The cove had once been a thriving pioneer settlement, now converted into a national park. An eleven-mile road wound through pastureland and woods. Historic buildings—hand-hewn log homes with rock chimneys, barns and outbuildings—were scattered through the park along the road and were open to exploration. Three churches still stood, their quiet interiors haunted by the echoes of psalms and sermons, their grounds the final resting place for generations of settlers.

The drive was Casey's idea. Natalie suspected that he was trying to keep her busy so she wouldn't worry so much about what was going on in Nashville. And it did help—to an extent.

After their drive, they returned to her cabin. Neither wanted to spend time with other people just then. Though they monitored their calls, they let most of them go to voice mail, not wanting anyone else to intrude on this precious time together.

"I like being with you," Casey murmured much later that day as they sprawled against her pillows, sated and happily exhausted.

Snuggling into his bare shoulder, she closed her eyes. "I like being with you, too."

"When this is over—when Andrew finds what he's looking for—"

Without opening her eyes, she frowned. "No," she said, cutting in before he could say anything else. "Let's not talk about that tonight. Let's just enjoy being together for now."

There was a taut moment of silence and she could tell he wanted to argue, but to her relief, he let it go. His arm tightened around her. "All right. We won't talk about it tonight. We'll wait."

A tense moment averted, she relaxed into his embrace again.

The call came late Tuesday as Casey and Natalie lingered over hamburgers he had cooked on the barbecue grill outside her cabin. Casey watched as Natalie checked the screen on her beeping cell phone, went very still for a moment, then lifted the phone to her ear. "Hello, Andrew."

Casey made no pretense of not listening to her side of the call, though she didn't say much. Andrew did most of the talking. It was obvious from Natalie's expression that she was shocked by whatever his cousin was saying to her.

"Are you sure?" she asked at one point. "Absolutely sure?"

Andrew must have answered affirmatively.

"All right," she said. "I'll see you tomorrow. Thank you, Andrew."

She closed her phone and looked rather blankly across the table at Casey.

"He solved your case?" Casey asked. "After only three days?"

He hoped it was true, of course. He wanted Natalie to be cleared as soon as possible. But after spending almost every minute of the past three days with her while she'd waited for a report from Andrew, Casey wasn't looking forward to saying goodbye to her when she went back to her own life.

She nodded, and he told himself he was glad.

"He said it wasn't really that difficult to solve. He said if the upper management of my firm had been more interested in finding out the truth than in covering up the potential scandal, they'd have hired someone themselves to look beyond the so-called evidence provided by their anonymous source. And he said Beecham was obviously milking me for every penny he could get without working all that hard on my behalf, or he would have come up with a name himself."

Casey could almost hear the tone of disgust in which Andrew had probably said those things. "Was it that Linski person? The one who's been spending all the money lately?"

She shook her head. "Andrew checked her out first thing. He said she's got a boyfriend. Older. Married. Willing to pay quite generously for a hot young woman to spend time with him while his wife takes regular trips to Europe and Las Vegas. A very obvious explanation, actually, and one Beecham should have easily found. Andrew thinks Beecham had a pretty good idea of where Cathy's money was coming from, but by keeping me focused on her, it made him look like he was making progress on my investigation."

He almost hated to ask the next question. "Was it your friend Amber?"

"No." There was both relief and lingering shock in her expression. "It was Thad."

"Thad? The guy you dated?"

Natalie nodded slowly. "He wanted money to keep up the extravagant lifestyle he's been living. He was approached by someone from the tabloids about one of the clients, a country music star in the middle of an ugly divorce, and he thought he could make a little extra cash by leaking some juicy information about the confidential terms of the divorce. He was so successful getting away with it that time that he became a regular source for the so-called reporter. And he found it easy enough to set me up to take the fall if someone figured out what was going on."

Casey wished he had the bastard in front of him now. His hands itched to do some damage to the jerk's probably pretty face. "How stupid was he to think he could get away with doing that to you?"

"He almost did get away with it," she pointed out, a glint of anger slowly replacing the shock in her eyes. "I can't imagine that he'd be stupid enough to try it again after letting me take the blame."

"How did Andrew find out it was him?"

"He didn't tell me the details—said he'd fill us in tomorrow when he brings the evidence I need to prove my innocence. But he tracked down the reporter and managed to 'persuade' him to give him Thad's name. Beecham had talked to the guy, but he wasn't as successful as Andrew at convincing him to reveal his source."

"Andrew does have his ways," Casey murmured. "What else did he find?"

"The reporter admitted that the checks were made out to me, but given to Thad. Andrew followed Thad around for a few hours and took some pictures of him with a woman who's apparently living with him now. Andrew thinks the woman probably posed as me and cashed the checks at various local banks. He said he could probably find at least one teller who remembers her. He has all the evidence I need to convince the senior partners that I have a very good case if I decide to make this fight messy and public. Thad's been caught. He just doesn't know it yet."

"Congratulations, Natalie. I'm glad it worked out for you." She still looked a little dazed. "I just wanted to clear my name."

"I know. Once you're back in your old job and Thad's gone, I'm sure everyone will realize that you were accused unfairly."

"I don't even know if I'll get my old job back. Herb and the other partners will probably still want me to quietly disappear."

"Yes, well, you have a little leverage on your side," he pointed out. "You have the means to embarrass them pretty thoroughly. Not to mention grounds for a lawsuit."

"So I should use extortion to get my job back?"

He shrugged. "Extortion. Justice. Call it what you wish."

She bit her lip, looking down at the half-eaten burger going cold on her plate. He figured she had lost her appetite. He knew he had.

"You said Andrew's coming tomorrow?"

She nodded. "He said he'd be here by noon. And he's bringing the report for me to take back to my firm."

"You'll want to do that soon, I assume."

"The sooner the better."

It was what he had expected her to say, but it still stung. "I don't blame you. I'd want my name cleared, too."

"I'm glad you understand."

"So we have one more night together."

A muscle jumped in her cheek, as if she had tightened her jaw. "Yes."

"Then we should make the most of it, shouldn't we? Are you through with your dinner?"

His matter-of-fact tone must have surprised her. "Um. Yes, I'm finished."

"Then how about we go enjoy that hot tub again?" he asked, beginning to clear the table.

She looked at him a moment, then gave him a misty smile. "I'll pour the wine."

Natalie watched as Casey put her suitcase in the trunk of her car and closed the lid. "Thanks," she said, tightening her fingers around the keys gripped in her hand.

"You're welcome. Are you sure you have everything?"

"Yes. I've been through the cabin three times. There's nothing left of mine in there."

She watched him swallow as he nodded. "Okay then."

She had already said her goodbyes to her aunt and uncle and to Molly and Kyle. She'd done so that morning before she'd returned to the cabin to load the car and say a more private farewell to Casey.

Putting that moment off just a bit longer, she knelt to pet the dog who sat at Casey's side, gazing up at her in what she would have sworn was anxious confusion. "You're going to be fine, Buddy," she said, her voice thick. "Casey's going to take care of you until he leaves and then you're going to live in Kyle and Molly's backyard. You'll like it there. The kids will love you and play with you. You'll probably even like playing with Poppy."

Buddy whined, sensing something in her voice he didn't

like. She rested her cheek on his head for a moment, then rose, ordering herself not to cry over parting with a dog. She wasn't even a dog person, she reminded herself.

"You're sure he'll be okay?" she asked Casey.

He nodded, his face grim. "I'll make sure that he is. I'm taking him to the vet tomorrow for his shots and then I'll introduce him to Kyle's family. You know they'll love him. He and Kyle already get along very well."

"I know. I just…"

"He'll be fine, Natalie."

She forced a smile. "Yes, of course he will be. Much better than living in the woods this winter, scrounging for a meal."

"Definitely better. Kyle and Molly have that big, fenced backyard and I'll buy a comfy, warm doghouse before I leave. He'll probably become Kyle's dog, since Kyle's never really bonded with Poppy."

She assured herself that was the best thing that could happen for Buddy. Kyle would take excellent care of the dog.

"I guess I'd better go, then," she said, shifting the keys again. She had a little over a four-hour drive ahead of her. She wanted to unpack, get a good night's sleep, and be prepared to stalk into Herb Schroeder's office first thing in the morning with the evidence that he had allowed himself to be thoroughly fooled.

She couldn't say she was looking forward to that confrontation, but she did anticipate seeing the look in his eyes when she presented him with the excellently documented evidence Andrew had put together for her. And when she left Herb's office, she intended to head straight for Thad's.

"You'll call me after you talk to them, right? I want to know everything they say."

She nodded. "I'll call you."

She had offered to pay Andrew for his services at the going

rate for a private investigator, but he'd refused, telling her he owed her this for his earlier, unauthorized invasion of her privacy. It wasn't even as if it had been all that difficult a case to solve, he'd added bluntly, making her feel a little stupid for letting Beecham dupe her for so long.

Like Casey, Andrew had expressed curiosity about what Herb said when she showed him what Andrew had found. He had also offered to talk to Herb personally if Natalie had any problems convincing the senior partner of the validity of her evidence. The reputation of his family firm back in Dallas was impeccable, and nationally respected, he'd added. He didn't expect any trouble from her bosses once they heard who she'd had on her side.

Casey placed his hands on her arms, rubbing slowly up and down as he gazed into her face. "I know you said you didn't want to talk about us until after your meeting with Schroeder..."

"Casey—"

"Is this really goodbye?" he insisted. "You're just going to go back to Nashville and forget about me?"

"I'm not going to forget about you," she told him quietly. "Ever. You got me through a very rough time. I will always appreciate that."

"You still think of me as a nice diversion?" he asked roughly.

She couldn't quite meet his eyes. "You know it was more than that."

"But you're still leaving."

"I have to, Casey. You know I have to clear my name. And you have a career to get back to in Dallas."

His hands gripped her shoulders. "You were more than a diversion to me, Natalie. A hell of a lot more."

She moistened her lips. "You said yourself you've been going through a tough time. You've been questioning your career and your goals, and you've recently broken up with your girlfriend."

"You're not a rebound affair, either," he said roughly. "Damn it."

"It's just not a good time for either of us to try to make this into more than we've had," she whispered.

She was sure that when he got home, back with his family and friends and the career he wanted despite the doubts he'd encountered lately, he would be relieved she hadn't tried to hold on to him. Besides, she knew herself too well. If she succeeded in getting her position back, or even if she found a job with another firm, it wouldn't be long until she was right back to her old ways of working too long and too hard, letting everything else in her life take second place to her career. That was no way to maintain any relationship, much less a long-distance one.

All of which sounded very logical. Very believable. But she suspected that the main reason she was running from Casey was fear—as much as she hated admitting that, even to herself. She'd been let down by too many people she had trusted lately. She wasn't ready to take the risk of being hurt that way again while she was still stinging from the last time.

It would hurt less to break it off now than to wait until his passion fizzled in the reality of too much distance and too little time.

"I've got to go," she said, steeling her resolve. "I'll call you tomorrow, I promise."

He nodded grimly. "Drive carefully."

"I will."

He lowered his head and kissed her until it was all she could do not to melt into a puddle at his feet. She had to put a hand on the car to steady herself when he finally drew away. "It wasn't a diversion," he said again, gruffly.

She looked into the rearview mirror as she drove away. Casey stood there watching her leave, his hand on the head of the dog who sat rather forlornly at his side.

For only the second time since she had been fired from her job, Natalie felt tears escape her eyes and trickle slowly down her cheeks.

Chapter Fourteen

As far as Casey was concerned, January was the cruelest month of the year. The holidays were over, leaving only scattered, once-festive, now-droopy decorations behind. The weather was almost unrelentingly gloomy, with gray skies, cold rain, occasional thunderstorms. Night fell early, so that it was usually dark by the time he got home from work.

Since his return from Tennessee seven weeks earlier, he'd thrown himself into the job with a renewed dedication, putting in long hours, showing up at the office for at least part of every day of the week to make up for all his time away. His superiors seemed reassured now that he had gotten his personal issues settled and he was prepared to be the valuable asset to the firm that they'd always expected him to become.

Even in the relatively short time that had passed since he'd returned, he'd accomplished a great deal in billable hours and out-of-court settlements. Because money had a way of soothing all fears in this business, he figured any remaining concerns about him would soon dissipate.

Tugging at the silk power-tie knotted at the throat of his tailored dress shirt, he walked off the elevator on his condo floor and sighed wearily. He'd had a great day, work-wise. Accomplished a real coup of a settlement with a case that could have stretched on for months. He should have been celebrating, but instead he was just…empty.

The feeling would go away, he assured himself. It was probably caused by the gloomy weather lately. Or post-holiday malaise—not that he'd particularly enjoyed the holidays this year, though he'd made an almost superhuman effort to conceal that from his family and friends.

He stopped walking when he saw someone sitting on the carpeted floor beside his door. "Aaron? What are you doing here?"

He didn't bother asking how his cousin had gotten into the secured building.

Aaron looked pointedly at his watch. "New superhero movie? Seven o'clock? The two of us were going to catch it tonight while Andy was busy with that surveillance job?"

"Oh, damn. I forgot. I'm sorry, I—"

"Forget it. Throw on a sweatshirt and some jeans and we'll go grab a burger."

"Yeah. That sounds good. Give me ten minutes." He unlocked his door and preceded his cousin inside.

"So how did your day go?" Aaron asked casually, glancing around Casey's immaculately decorated, fashionably neutral living room.

Casey pulled off his tie and shrugged out of his jacket. "It was good. Negotiated a very profitable settlement that could have gotten sticky."

"Congratulations. That must have felt good."

"I guess." He was already unbuttoning his shirt as he headed for the bedroom.

Aaron tagged after him. "You don't sound exactly elated. Tired?"

"Yeah, I guess so." Bone tired, he thought, pulling a pair of jeans and a Texas Longhorns sweatshirt out of the closet. Soul tired. Heart tired.

"Dude, you're killing me."

Tossing his shirt on the bed, Casey looked questioningly at his cousin, who was leaning in the bedroom doorway. "What are you talking about?"

"I can't stand to see you this glum. You've been this way ever since you got back from Tennessee, though you've done a really good job of hiding it."

Casey tugged the sweatshirt over his head. "I'll get over it."

"Get over what?"

"You're the one who started this. What do *you* think?"

"I think you didn't really want to come back from Gatlinburg," Aaron said bluntly.

Turning his back to the doorway, Casey swapped his suit pants for comfortably faded jeans. "Does anyone ever really want a vacation to end?"

"It's more than that, Case."

Turning back to his cousin, Casey released a long sigh. "I miss Natalie," he admitted, the first time he'd said it out loud since he'd parted from her almost two months earlier. "I even miss the dog."

"Have you tried calling? Natalie, not the dog."

"I haven't spoken to her since she called to let me know she'd gotten her position back with the firm in Nashville."

"How do you know she isn't missing you, too?"

"She's the one who said it wouldn't work between us. If she'd changed her mind, she knew how to reach me."

"So you're just going to spend the rest of your life trudging back and forth to work, pretending to be happy?"

"Give me a break, Aaron. I'm trying, okay?"

Aaron smiled sympathetically. "You're trying too hard. It shouldn't be this difficult."

"So what do *you* think I should do?" Casey challenged, seriously hoping for an answer.

"I think you should figure out what it takes to make you happy. And then do it."

"You make it sound so damned easy."

"I never said it was easy. Heck, I'm still trying to decide what *I* want to do for the rest of my life. I just know it's got to be something that makes me look forward to getting up in the morning. Something I can be proud of. Something that reflects who I am and what makes me happy."

Aaron had always been the more philosophical of the cousins. The one more prone to expressing his thoughts and emotions. The one who was always the most curious about what was around the next corner, most open to experience and change. Which probably explained why he'd tried half a dozen different jobs already in his short working life, Casey thought wryly. But Aaron always seemed to know what he wanted, even if he hadn't quite found it yet. Casey realized he should try a bit harder to emulate his younger cousin. He needed to figure out once and for all what *he* wanted—and then go after it, despite the risk of disappointment or failure.

But did he really have the courage to walk away from his life here again? For good this time?

There were patches of snow on the sides of the roads when Natalie drove up the mountain toward the cabin. She was lucky that the temperatures had been high enough the day before to melt the snow on the roads, though she'd been warned to keep an eye out for icy spots in the shade.

She was also fortunate that the cabin had been available for this impulsive weekend visit. She wouldn't have put it past her aunt and uncle to rearrange any existing reservations on her behalf, but Aunt Jewel had assured her that they really had gotten a cancellation for the cabin. She'd sounded delighted when Natalie said she'd like to spend a couple of nights there to celebrate her thirtieth birthday.

Natalie felt a little guilty for treating herself to a solitary birthday celebration. Her mother had wanted her to come to Mississippi for the occasion, but she had demurred. After all, she'd spent Christmas there with her mother and stepfather, and though she'd had a pleasant enough time, she wasn't eager to go back so soon.

Instead, she was going to spend her thirtieth birthday torturing herself with painful memories, as she had been for the past lonely weeks. She'd spent entirely too much time looking at the photographs she had taken of Casey, missing him, wondering if he was missing her. She'd rubbed the little broken-heart-shaped rock she'd picked up by the creek until she'd practically left fingerprints embedded in the smooth surface. And sometime during the past month or so, she had decided it was time for a major life change. She needed an evening of relaxation, a quiet walk in the woods, and a soothing soak in the hot tub to brace herself for all the questions to come.

Except for the random patches of snow, the cabin looked exactly as she remembered it. She bit her lip as the memories swept over her, making her wonder if she had made a mistake coming back here.

She slid out of her car and shut the driver's door, deciding to bring her bags in a little later. She had taken two steps toward the front door of the cabin, when the sound of a dog barking stopped her in her tracks.

Surely that wasn't… ?

Drawn irresistibly toward the sound, she rounded the end of the cabin and looked toward the stream at the back of the property. Her breath caught in her throat when she saw the reddish-brown and white dog loping toward her, his tail wagging in frantic welcome. "Buddy?"

The dog stood on his back legs, propping his front feet against her as he tried to lick her face. Laughing, she leaned down to hug him, not even caring that he was getting mud all over her jeans and coat. "What are you doing here?" she demanded, as if he could answer. "I hope you haven't run away again."

"Actually, he's with me."

She looked up slowly, her heart starting to pound so hard it made her a little dizzy. Keeping a hand on the dog to steady herself, she straightened, looking at the man who smiled at her from only a few feet away. "Casey."

"Hi, Natalie."

"I…can't believe you're here. I wasn't expecting you."

"I know. I hope it's a good surprise."

"But—how did you know?"

He laughed briefly. "Do you really have to ask? Molly told me you were going to be here."

"Oh. Of course she did. So, why…?"

He took a step closer, his eyes locked with hers, the expression in his eyes achingly tender. "Damn, but I've missed you," he said roughly. "I was planning to come to Nashville next week to see you, but when Molly told me you were coming here, I knew this was the right place to find you again."

"You were coming to Nashville?" She was having a hard

time thinking clearly, probably because of the shock of having him near her again. So close she had only to take a couple of steps to be in his arms. Almost quivering with the desire to take those steps, she asked, "Why?"

"Because I've missed you so much it's been tearing me apart. I had to find out if there was any way I could change your mind about giving us another chance. You thought I was in a vulnerable place the last time we were together, maybe on the rebound, not in a position to know what I wanted. And maybe I wondered if you were right. Maybe that's why I left without fighting harder to change your mind, because I needed to know for sure what I wanted."

He shook his head firmly. "Well, it's been almost two months now, Natalie, and my feelings haven't changed. I still want to be with you. I'm prepared to do whatever it takes to convince you of how good we are together, even if it means moving to Nashville and finding a position there while you make up your mind."

"That…wouldn't do you any good," she said unsteadily.

His eyes darkened and he seemed to brace himself for rejection. "You're telling me there's no chance?"

She swallowed, shaken by the raw emotion she saw in his face. "No. I'm telling you I don't live in Nashville any longer. Or I won't, after my lease runs out at the end of next month. I've already turned in my resignation at the firm."

Frowning, he asked, "You quit?"

She nodded. "I quit."

What might have been hope brightened his eyes again. He took another step closer. "Why?"

"Because I wanted more out of life than working myself into the ground to satisfy people who had been so willing to believe the worst of me. People who didn't really care about me outside the money I could make for them, who only accepted me back among them because they were afraid I'd cause trouble for them if they didn't. I still want a rewarding and satisfying career, and I want it to be in the field I've trained for—but I don't want that to be the only thing in my life. I want more."

"Funny," he said huskily. "I've been thinking much the same way lately. I'm tired of being a drone in a corporate hive. I want to walk my own path."

"Is that path wide enough for two?" she asked in a whisper.

He closed his eyes for just a moment, then opened them again and reached for her. "Oh, yeah."

She emerged from the kiss a long time later, flushed and tousled and happier than she could ever remember. "I was going to come to you," she confessed. "I debated whether to call you or just show up in Dallas, but I'd finally decided on the latter. I wanted to see your face when I asked you if you still felt the same way I did."

He looked delighted by her admission. "You were coming to Dallas?"

"I already have the plane reservations."

Laughing, he hugged her tightly. "You can use them, anyway. I want you to meet my family."

The thought of meeting all those people he had described to her made her mouth go dry, but she nodded. "I'd like to meet them."

He covered her mouth with his again. Buddy bounced around them, happily welcoming them back.

After finally emerging for air, Natalie smiled down at the dog. "He seems happy to see us."

"He is. Kyle said he's given them no problems and he seemed content enough living with them, but he went nuts when he saw me. It was almost like he was asking what took me so long to come back for him. He seems to feel the same way about you, judging by how happy he looks to see you."

"I'm glad to see him, too." She ruffled the dog's silky ears. "I missed you, Buddy. Maybe you've turned me into a dog person, after all."

"Hey, Nat?" Casey asked, his voice husky again.

She smiled besottedly up at him. "Yes?"

"I'm freezing. Want to go inside?"

"Okay." She reached up to stroke a fingertip down his cheek. "We could check out the hot tub again. Just to make sure it's still working correctly, of course."

"I've always liked the way you think," he murmured, catching her hand and placing a kiss against it. He tucked her snugly against him as they turned together toward the cabin, then looked back over his shoulder. "Come on, Buddy."

Natalie rested her chin on her crossed hands on Casey's bare, still rapidly rising-and-falling chest, gazing thoughtfully up at him. "So," she asked, "where are we going to hang our shingle? Texas or Tennessee? Or somewhere in between?"

He opened his eyes with a rough laugh. "You want to talk about work now?"

She smiled. "It was just a passing thought while we, um, recover our strength."

Stroking her hair, he lifted his other arm and slid his hand beneath his head, getting comfortable. "It doesn't really matter to me where we are, as long as it's together. Either way, one of us is going to have to get licensed to practice in another state."

"That's true."

After a moment, he said, "You know, I've actually been giving this some thought the past few days, ever since I came to the conclusion that I wanted to make a big change in my life. A change that included you, of course," he added.

She smiled.

"You know I'm close to my family. I've never lived more than a few miles away from my parents, my cousins."

"Texas, then," she said with a shrug. It truly didn't matter to her, she realized in a sort of wonder.

"No, that's not what I meant. I think it's time I strike out on my own a little more. I'll always be close to my family, and I'll want to visit them often—but I think I should follow Molly's example and move away for a while. I think it would be good for me."

"So…where?"

"I could be very happy in this area," he admitted. "I love it here. Maybe we could set up a small practice here in East Tennessee."

"I love it here, too. I always have. Of course, we both still have family here, so it's not like we'd be totally separated from them."

"That's not such a bad thing, either. At least we won't be right in the middle of my whole clan. We'll have room to breathe, freedom to establish our own routines and boundaries."

"I like the sound of that."

"So do I. It'll be a challenge, of course. Starting a new practice is going to be expensive and risky. It's going to be a while before we see much profit."

"I've always enjoyed a challenge."

He chuckled. "So have I. Maybe that's why I was drawn so strongly to you."

"Mmm. So…what will it be? Lofton and Walker? Or Walker and Lofton?"

"So you're keeping your maiden name? After we're married, I mean? That's fine with me, if it's what you want, I'm just—"

"Wait a minute." She lifted her head, staring at him. "We're getting married?"

"Sooner or later," he said with a grin. "I'd prefer sooner, but I'll settle for however long it takes me to convince you. I'm interested in much more than a business partnership with you, Natalie. I want it all. I love you."

"Oh."

Her rational, logical mind immediately filled with all the reasons they shouldn't be talking about this yet. It was too soon. They hadn't known each other long enough. They should probably work together for a while, maybe live together to make sure it would all work out.

But when it came right down to it, there was only one thing that really mattered. "I love you, too."

Casey drew her upward to seal that sentiment with a long, thorough kiss.

She decided to worry about the details later. The new Natalie wasn't ruled by doubts and fears and other people's expectations. She went after what she wanted without hesitation. And she very much wanted the life she and Casey had just envisioned together.

Out on the warm, soft hearth rug, Buddy sighed contentedly and settled in for a cozy winter's night sleep.

HARLEQUIN® Romance®

This February the Harlequin® Romance series
will feature six Diamond Brides stories featuring
diamond proposals and gorgeous grooms.

Share your dream wedding proposal and you could WIN!

The most romantic entry will win a diamond
necklace and will inspire a proposal in one of
our upcoming Diamond Grooms books in 2010.

In 100 words or less, tell us the most romantic
way that you dream of being proposed to.

For more information, and to enter
the Diamond Brides Proposal contest, please visit
www.DiamondBridesProposal.com

Or mail your entry to us at:
IN THE U.S.: 3010 Walden Ave., P.O. Box 9069, Buffalo, NY 14269-9069
IN CANADA: 225 Duncan Mill Road, Don Mills, ON M3B 3K9

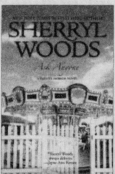

REQUEST YOUR FREE BOOKS!

2 FREE NOVELS PLUS 2 FREE GIFTS!

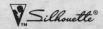

SPECIAL EDITION®

Life, Love and Family!

YES! Please send me 2 FREE Silhouette Special Edition® novels and my 2 FREE gifts (gifts are worth about $10). After receiving them, if I don't wish to receive any more books, I can return the shipping statement marked "cancel." If I don't cancel, I will receive 6 brand-new novels every month and be billed just $4.24 per book in the U.S. or $4.99 per book in Canada, plus 25¢ shipping and handling per book and applicable taxes, if any*. That's a savings of at least 15% off the cover price! I understand that accepting the 2 free books and gifts places me under no obligation to buy anything. I can always return a shipment and cancel at any time. Even if I never buy another book from Silhouette, the two free books and gifts are mine to keep forever.

235 SDN EEYU   335 SDN EEY6

Name _____ (PLEASE PRINT) _____

Address _____ Apt. # _____

City _____ State/Prov. _____ Zip/Postal Code _____

Signature (if under 18, a parent or guardian must sign)

Mail to the **Silhouette Reader Service:**
IN U.S.A.: P.O. Box 1867, Buffalo, NY 14240-1867
IN CANADA: P.O. Box 609, Fort Erie, Ontario L2A 5X3

Not valid to current subscribers of Silhouette Special Edition books.

Want to try two free books from another line?
Call 1-800-873-8635 or visit www.morefreebooks.com.

* Terms and prices subject to change without notice. N.Y. residents add applicable sales tax. Canadian residents will be charged applicable provincial taxes and GST. Offer not valid in Quebec. This offer is limited to one order per household. All orders subject to approval. Credit or debit balances in a customer's account(s) may be offset by any other outstanding balance owed by or to the customer. Please allow 4 to 6 weeks for delivery. Offer available while quantities last.

Your Privacy: Silhouette is committed to protecting your privacy. Our Privacy Policy is available online at www.eHarlequin.com or upon request from the Reader Service. From time to time we make our lists of customers available to reputable third parties who may have a product or service of interest to you. If you would prefer we not share your name and address, please check here. ☐

SSE08R

The Inside Romance newsletter has a NEW look for the new year!

Same great content, brand-new look!

The Inside Romance newsletter is a FREE quarterly newsletter highlighting our upcoming series releases and promotions!

Click on the Inside Romance link on the front page of **www.eHarlequin.com** or e-mail us at insideromance@harlequin.ca to sign up to receive your FREE newsletter today!

You can also subscribe by writing to us at: HARLEQUIN BOOKS Attention: Customer Service Department P.O. Box 9057, Buffalo, NY 14269-9057

Please allow 4-6 weeks for delivery of the first issue by mail.

IRNNEW09